Other books by Haley Cass

Those Who Wait

Forever and A Day

When You Least Expect It

In the Long Run

Down to A Science

Dedication and Acknowledgements

As always, an amazing thank you to my friends who support my crazy self whenever I'm writing any project. Kate, Kuver, Monica, Luke, and Alina in particular for this project – in the immortal words of Lizzie McGuire, you rock don't ever change.

Much like how When You Least Expect It came to exist because someone else essentially talked me into writing it... this story also does. Thank you, Rachael, for being the most inspiring person for me. The one who listens to every idea I have and rarely laughs whenever I say "hey... I have a new idea." I love you and I appreciate everything, always.

But the most special of notes in this companion novel in particular, goes to all of my patrons. This novella was first written and published on my patreon a year ago as my Christmas special, and the incredible support and wonderful people there make writing feel doubly as amazing as it already feels (which, for the record, is a lot). This literally wouldn't have been written without you.

Specifically, Angie Bobinger, Bridget Ruane, Crystal McKinney, Hana Huskovic, Nicola Lewis, Rachel, Alice Schruba, Betsy Walker, Carrie Totta, Cora Linehan, rb, Dalene Englebrecht, Hillary Manns, Jacqueline Reed, Jo Cobain, Kasey, Larissa Frank, Regina A, Sarah Baker-Goldsmith, and Ricci. The best of the best of the best.

Copyright © 2022 Haley Cass

All rights reserved.

The characters and events portrayed in this book are fictitious. Any similarity to real persons, living or dead, is coincidental and not intended by the author.

No part of this book may be reproduced, or stored in a retrieval system, or transmitted in any form or by any means, electronic, mechanical, photocopying, recording, or otherwise, without express written permission of the publisher.

ISBN-13: 9798360556480

Cover Artist: Cath Grace Designs

Printed in the United States of America

Special Foreword:

Happiest of holidays, gentle readers!

I started my journey with *When You Least Expect It*, intending for it to be a simple holiday novella. But, as I started writing Caroline and Hannah (and Abbie), I fell in love with them and realized… I couldn't write their journey in so few words. Their love story was a *love story* and it deserved to be told with the proper amount of time for them to fall in love.

Mostly, though, I realized – while Caroline was going to fall for Hannah relatively quickly, within a few months, it would take longer for Hannah to be able to get there with Caroline.

I thought *When You Least Expect It* worked the best as one linear story from a single point of view, and I still believe that. But I also think that Hannah had her own journey – a big journey – that had to be told.

A journey about the lows someone can reach and how rewarding it can be to pull yourself out of them, maybe with a helping hand along the way. About how maybe falling in love can be terrifying, but hopefully it can be worth it.

… all of this to say, I hope you have read *When You Least Expect It* before this! Welcome to Hannah's point of view.

December 21 – 8 Years Ago

"*You* and my granddaughter are coming over on Christmas Eve, right?" Hannah's mom, Betty, asked. "I feel like it's been way too long since I've seen those cute little cheeks. And Abbie's too."

Hannah rolled her eyes even as she smiled. "Mom, you literally saw us *both* three days ago."

"Barely! You two coming by the diner and having dinner with me on my break doesn't count."

"I can't believe you're saying that the drawing Abbie gave you at dinner didn't count! We are going to have to demand it back."

"You can pry it out of my desperately in-need-of-a-manicure hands, then, can't you?" Her mom cleared her throat as she walked and Hannah could hear how fast she was moving. A sign of her hustling to work for the breakfast shift, bright and early. "Abbie did love seeing them cook, though, the last time she came to work with me."

"Mom! You let her in the kitchen?"

She could practically hear her mom's eyeroll. "Honey, you think you weren't raised in that kitchen? Come on. Speaking of, I'm about to clock in, so I've gotta go."

She could only shake her head, because… well, her mom was right. She'd spent more time than she could ever recount everywhere in the diner. It didn't mean she wanted her daughter toddling around back there, though. Hannah had the small scar on the back of her neck, still, from when she'd thought the kitchen was her personal playground and she'd accidentally knocked one of the pots down from the open flame stove as she'd been running by it, and it had sizzled against her skin as she'd passed it.

"Okay, I'll let you go. And please," she lowered her voice in deference to her mom, knowing how much she always *hated* Hannah mentioning this, "If you need anything for rent or bills next month, could you please ask me instead of working seventy hours a week? Seriously. Those are whole days you could spend with Abbie and me," she added, trying to convince her. Desperately trying. It wasn't the first time this had been a conversation and she was certain it wouldn't be the last.

"You don't have to take care of me, Banana. I'm just fine," came her mom's unsurprising response.

Just fine mostly, sure. But Hannah could already see the toll working so much had taken on her mom as she neared sixty. And she didn't like to see it, not one bit. Especially not when she had the access to money to do actually something about it, now.

She bit her lip; on one hand, hating an argument, especially about money, but on the other… "Mom–"

"Christmas Eve. Michael can come. Or not," Betty offered, her tone light and playful, but Hannah knew she wasn't kidding. "I love you."

Betty Woodland was a force of nature. Someone who could do anything based on sheer willpower, Hannah had always thought so. It was something that, at twenty-four, Hannah could still only admire; she didn't have that innate quality.

"Love you, too, Mom." She held the phone out for Abbie, who sporadically had been watching her from across the room while also eating/playing with her oatmeal and fruit. "Say goodbye to gram, Ab."

"Bye gram-gram! Love you!" Abbie's adorable smile beamed across the room as she clapped her oatmeal-y hands together.

She hung up the phone, breathing out a deep sigh regarding her mom's "invitation" for Michael.

It hadn't taken Hannah long to realize that the fairytale forever she'd naively thought she'd been handed wasn't all it was cracked up to be.

It just, unfortunately, took *too* long.

Because now, she'd already dropped out of college and was living solely off of Michael, they were married, and she already had Abbie.

So… perhaps she got the feeling in her gut that Michael perhaps wasn't being entirely honest with her about where he was going or who he was with. Then again, maybe she was – as he would often accuse her – being paranoid.

And maybe Michael could control his temper more or the way he spoke to her. Perhaps she wished that she could ever even *try* to bring up her issues without being snapped or yelled at.

But, it wasn't as though he hit her and it wasn't like the bad stuff happened every single day, either.

And so, maybe she wished that he was more involved with Abbie than he was, given that he was rarely ever home and when he was, the last thing he wanted was to be "bothered" by their two-year-old.

Which, Hannah just couldn't understand at all, because Abbie was a wonder to her, every single day. She was constantly growing and learning and exploring, all the while being the cutest toddler to ever exist.

Two and a half years in, and… no, her marriage wasn't a fairytale. Then again, she told herself for the hundredth time, marriages weren't fairytales. *That was something she'd learned in the last few years –*

Hannah had been so intent in high school, at the urging of her mom, to focus on school. Get good grades. Do the extra-curriculars. Get into college. Work hard to have the life she wanted. Relationships would always be there, later. The right person would be there, later, to sweep her off her feet when everything was just right.

She'd been foolish to believe that. That at *any* point, a relationship would come along when things were *just right*. It had been easy to let herself get swept away in Michael when she'd met him at twenty. Handsome, so smart, so charismatic, so *interested*. So much money that he might be even richer than real princes? A prince charming.

It just... it just took her until really being married to learn that marriages weren't fairytales at all, and no man was really a prince charming. *This* was what it was like. What she had, was reality.

So, reality wasn't a fairytale, but – at least she wasn't holding onto that naivety even longer in her life.

And Michael was right – she didn't ever have to struggle to pay for anything, her daughter never experienced what she went through as a child when she'd seen her mother stress herself to the bone trying to figure out how all of the bills were going to get paid or ducking down under the windowsill when they saw the water or electric companies park outside. She got to spend her days raising her daughter and experiencing every little moment with her. *That* was a blessing.

When Hannah had been younger, her mom would always focus on the positive side and tell her they would "make the best of it."

So, Hannah was "making the best of" her marriage, as much as she could. And generally, most days, it was – it was fine. It was just fine.

Not that her mother would ever want to hear about her *making the best of* her marriage. There was a reason her mom had always kicked her romantic interests to the curb at slightest transgressions. After Hannah's dad had left them high and dry when she'd been four, Hannah's mom had been very focused on making sure that the two of them would never *settle*, again.

Perhaps that was where Hannah had gotten those unrealistic romance expectations of her youth.

No, her mother didn't hide any of her feelings about Michael at all, and they weren't pleasant. She understood that; it was also... fine.

Hannah hummed along to the Christmas music on the radio, smiling at the way Abbie kicked her feet out where she sat at her booster seat and sang along in half made-up words as well.

She continued to mix her sugar cookie dough, only realizing Michael entered the kitchen when he sighed loudly behind her.

She spun around, fixing on a smile in spite of the aggravated look on his face. Marriage was all a learning curve, but something she'd learned very early was that if she could get Michael off to work in a decent mood, then she could look forward to a better evening when he came home.

"Good morning. How'd you sleep?"

"Fine. Tired, still," he grunted back, adjusting his tie as he took in the kitchen.

Hannah bit the inside of her cheek as she looked down at the bowl and continued to mix. "Yes, well, you got in a bit late, so I can imagine."

She did her best to temper her tone and not sound too inquisitive or, worse, accusatory. She never really even meant to sound accusing, but apparently, sometimes she did. And Michael did not appreciate those times. But his last secretary had quit so suddenly and had showed up at their house to yell at Michael only three weeks ago, so it was on Hannah's mind, still. In spite of Michael's seemingly-heartfelt assurances that nothing had happened.

"What the hell is going on in here?" He stepped closer, narrowing his eyes into the bowl. "First thing in the morning and you're making dessert?"

"I made you a coffee and put it in your to-go thermos with your briefcase and jacket, in the mudroom," she informed him, tone light. Not only did she not want to spark another fight in general, but she hated whenever it happened in front of Abbie. She knew, as Michael always said, that she was so young, she wouldn't remember but… Hannah didn't want to take any chances.

Michael was close enough that she could smell his aftershave and fresh cologne after his shower.

She could feel the deep breath he took in. And her stomach was littered with nerves.

"But what are you doing? Shouldn't you be getting ready for tonight? This Christmas party is important. Junior partner is only a stepping stone, and Wilkens is going to be taking note of *everything*. We have to impress – the both of us."

Hannah bit back a sigh, her nerves just barely lightening at the fact that this wasn't an immediate fight.

Marriage was a learning curve, she thought again, especially when you married far beyond your own social and financial class. That was also something she was still adjusting to. The way to work a room at a function, the right designers to wear, the committees to join as a housewife, what topics to bring up at dinner parties.

His face darkened, his eyes going out of focus in the way they did that did calm her a bit. It meant he was upset at something or someone else, and not her. "Especially now that they hired *Parker*. I swear, Granger is so up her ass, and she's trying to put on this act and try to charm as many people as possible before they see right through her."

Hannah nodded to placate him. This was far from the first rant she'd heard about Caroline Parker, the new hire at the firm a couple of months ago. The woman who had come in and had been given some of Michael's cases and bungled them. A reason he'd had to stay late for several weeks in a row. Then they'd had to work together on a handful of cases, in which Caroline had messed up a bunch of small details that Michael was left to fix – causing even more late nights.

Some weekends.

This wasn't even to speak about the horrendous attitude and rude behaviors she'd heard about.

Ice bitch was Michael's preferred term, though there were many. Hannah… didn't love them, but it wasn't usually worth a fight that directed the attitude her way.

And so, she fixed on a small smile and turned to look at him. "Of course, I remember the party, Michael. I'm on the events committee at your firm," she reminded, managing to hold back her sigh. "And these cookies are *for* the party."

The frown on his face deepened, though. It was less of his angry look now, and more of a confused annoyance. Much better. She could manage that. "Then why are you baking? Shouldn't you just leave that to the caterers? I mean, Hannah, come on. This sort of thing is what we pay people for."

Hannah grit her teeth and cut her eyes toward Abbie. God, the last thing she wanted was for Abbie to grow up thinking like that. Her daughter seemed to be paying absolutely no mind to them, thankfully.

"I think it offers your company a nice personal touch. Something like that could set you apart from other people," she spoke lightly. And she wanted to do it. She wanted to have something else to do and to offer, other than simply hanging from Michael's arm.

That conversation hadn't gone over well the last time, though.

He tilted his head in consideration, before giving a curt nod. "Well, as long as it doesn't detract from the time you're going to spend getting ready." Michael flashed the charming smile she'd fallen for. It was less charming, now, but she still could see what she'd fallen for a few years ago; it was just like a perfect toothpaste commercial kind of smile. "Gotta show everyone how I married up."

Hannah managed another small, tight grin at him as he kissed her cheek, drawing in a deep breath before she turned around and reached up to straighten his collar. "Don't worry. I'll be ready on time; have I ever not been?"

Michael was in a notably better mood now as he stepped back. "Perfect." He checked his watch. "I better be going. I'll see you tonight."

He turned to stride right back out of the room, without another look, which –

"Aren't you going to say good morning to Abbie before you go?" There was steel in her tone now, but this was the tone she couldn't control. Not when it came to Abbie.

She didn't miss the way his shoulders tensed in that way he got when he was annoyed, but he did turn and redirect to give a brief greeting to their daughter, who excitedly grinned at him with the attention.

No fairytale, but it was okay. And Abbie, well, she was much better than okay.

***

As promised, Hannah arrived at the Christmas party, cookies in tow, not only on-time, but early. Being prompt was always important to her.

She'd slipped on the designer dress she'd bought and had been on Michael's arm right at the beginning of the event, circling the room with him. Hannah thought she was getting pretty good at making those rounds, if she did say so herself.

Sometimes she struggled with… words. With saying the right thing to the right people, feeling put on the spot. That had always made her feel tongue-tied, even more so after getting married to Michael – it was in the way he was so quick with his words, so easily running circles around her with any hint of dissatisfaction in her tone, as if he was arguing the most intense legal case in a courtroom, that made her feel jumbled, made her feel… silly, and stupid.

But the trick at these events, she'd learned, was to remind herself that none of this was really *her*. When she reminded herself that this was all a role she was playing – of a perfect housewife, who lived a false fairytale – the words came easier, then.

The worst part of these events, she'd come to know, wasn't even having to put on the show for Michael's bosses and the higher-ups.

It was, honestly, when Michael was done with her.

He referred to it as mingling – but the kind he had to do alone. Sometimes he disappeared, even, from the party. He often reported going to the bosses' offices and having a drink or a cigar with some of the other men. And even if that was true, it didn't help that Hannah felt like old leftovers for most of the night, after she'd been taken around the room and shown off. Like she was cast-off. Discarded.

Like she was nothing. Nothing more than quite literally the pretty face Michael enjoyed showing off.

She'd attempted, for the first year and a half of these parties and events, to do her own mingling, as Michael often encouraged, with the other wives. But, of course, there were rules to that, too.

Not every wife was someone she was supposed to mingle with. Only women married to men that *Michael* wanted to socialize with. Otherwise, her bonding could lead to him having to spend time with someone he didn't want to "waste time" with.

And as much as Hannah didn't want to be… well, this kind of woman, generally, the wives that Michael wanted her to socialize with – they weren't exactly the company she wanted to keep. First and foremost, because Hannah was not from their world, and they knew it. But how many times could she talk about fashion, when she thought spending thousands of dollars on a single dress was utterly ludicrous and such a waste?

She'd learned very quickly to keep that thought to herself.

It was about that time of night, though. The time where Hannah was left to her own devices, smiling when people made eye contact, while Michael disappeared. She leaned into the corner of the room she'd claimed as her own, sipping lightly on the champagne Michael had absently handed her a while ago. She didn't need to be told, though, not to have more than one glass. She knew Michael's rules of work functions.

She wondered how Abbie was doing with her grandparents for the night and contemplated calling, even though she knew the look she would get when Michael found out.

Still, she stepped forward, intending to take a breather and make the call when she saw the woman at the refreshment table that was home to Hannah's cookies.

She'd been pretty displeased with the way Michael had essentially tossed them aside without even a look at the caterers. And many of the women he wanted her to socialize with weren't going to eat those cookies, anyway, it was true.

This woman was, though. She was eating one, with two others on a little plate. And unlike a lot of the other women here, she wasn't in a dress; she was wearing an impeccably tailored red suit.

It fit her perfectly, highlighting shapely hips and a chest much more generous than Hannah's own.

It was her face that caught Hannah's attention, though. Sometimes, Hannah got hit with the itch to draw – usually, admittedly, it was an urge to draw architecture. If she was outside in nature and saw something gripping, she itched to draw that, too. She rarely wanted to draw people.

But this woman's face was absolutely striking.

She was very pretty, yes, but it was the sharp lines of her face that made Hannah feel like it would be *perfect* to draw. Sharp cheekbones, a small, sloped nose, perfectly arched eyebrows. The symmetry of her was… enthralling.

Offset by a dark freckle under her left eye and the dimple next to her mouth on the right side.

Sharp lines, perfect symmetry, but offset just enough to be interesting.

Without conscious thought, she was walking over to her, wanting just a closer look at her face, before she found herself next to the woman.

Striking, Hannah thought again, pleased that this face was even more aesthetically enjoyable up close. There was a little crinkle in her cheek, right next to that dimple, visible here. Yeah, she really wanted to draw that.

It was only when she realized how close she stood that she cursed herself. She had nothing to actually say and now… Hannah opened her mouth but – damningly – had none of the words to strike up a conversation.

"Are you enjoying those?" Was what finally escaped her mouth when she was able to latch onto something.

The woman spun to face her, eyes widening as she started coughing, choking on the bite of the cookie she'd just taken. The small smile Hannah had felt playing on her lips dropped at the reaction and she uselessly fluttered her hands in front of her before she interlocked her fingers to make herself stop looking like a total idiot as the coughing came to an end.

Her eyes were endlessly dark, and Hannah's own searched them, before they flicked over the rest of her. The woman's hair matched the color of those eyes, exactly. A rich, dark brown. Cut sharply to frame her jaw, with natural waves that softened the look a little. Just enough to offset all of that sharpness, the thought rang around in her head once more.

Quite possibly the most perfect face in the world. Her fingers itched for a pencil. Or to trace those sharp lines.

"I'm – yeah, they're actually amazing," the woman eventually answered. "And this is coming from someone who normally doesn't love sugar cookies in spite of a serious love affair with both sugar and cookies." Her voice dropped to a playful whisper.

Hannah could tell from the way the woman's eyes twinkled and a smile tugged at her lips, that she didn't suffer from the same affliction of never being able to find the right fucking words.

But she didn't feel the same sort of awkwardness with this woman that she usually did with people at these events. Maybe it was because of the easy stance she had or the inviting look she gave.

Maybe her compliment to Hannah's baking also had something to do with it. Michael frequently complained about how much "time she wasted" by cooking and baking, and though he was happy to eat the meals she made, he also made comments about how he wanted to hire someone to cook for them.

This woman's very clear enjoyment of her cookies made her cheeks feel warm, and she couldn't help but smile. "I won't tell anyone. But as the person who made them, I'm feeling pretty pleased."

It was so silly to feel as satisfied as she did when those dark eyes widened, the woman looking from her plate to Hannah, honestly like she was some sort of goddess. Abbie was maybe the only person who appreciated her cooking so much, but getting the approval from her toddler didn't feel quite the same.

"You made these? I assumed it was all catered…" She trailed off, the warmth in her gaze making Hannah's cheeks heat.

And her smile grew, uncontrollably. "Most of it is, actually. But I'm on the event council for the firm and I just figured… why not contribute a bit?"

The woman snorted, "You're contributing terrible things to my self-control."

The outright mischievousness in her eyes made Hannah feel easily more relaxed than she'd felt all night. More than she ever felt at these events, really. "I think this time of year is just about when everyone's self-control takes a dive."

With a head tilt and a warm look in her eye, the woman opened her mouth to speak, only to shut it a second later, her eyes focusing over Hannah's shoulder. Her entire demeanor changed; the easy, joking set of her shoulders tightening as if she was getting ready to go to war.

Hannah didn't even have to turn as she felt Michael approach. She could smell the cologne and feel his touch slide over the small of her back as he stepped close enough to brush against her. "Hannah, dear," his hand tightened at her waist, the grip bruising, making it just difficult enough to stop her smile from turning to a grimace. "What are you doing with Caroline?"

The next couple of minutes passed in a shocked blur for her, because… this was Caroline? The striking woman who loved her cookies and made her feel at ease was *Caroline*? The same one Michael ranted and raved about, the one who was rude and cold and incompetent?

"What the hell were you doing talking to her?" Michael hissed in her ear as soon as Caroline had walked away, and Hannah followed her with her eyes. Hannah's eyes just seemed to want to be on her, even though she was… Caroline. "What did she want from you? Was she hitting on you?"

That jarred her out of her stunned stupor, and she leaned back enough to look up at him. "What? Hitting on me?"

"She's a dyke, Hannah," Michael snarled.

She winced as the word hit her ears, pulling back even more from his embrace, even as his hand tightened, digging harder into her. "Cut it out. She wasn't hitting on me; we were talking about cookies. And don't say that word, it's rude."

Michael was glaring toward where Caroline had disappeared into the crowd. He was far too fixated on her to fixate on Hannah. "Well, she was probably only seconds away from it. Look at you. Of course she was. On my wife."

Hannah vaguely wondered if it would have sounded like *she* was hitting on *Caroline* had she been able to ask the words that she desperately wished she could – if she could draw her. The thought made her want to laugh, but she knew she absolutely couldn't smile in the face of Michael's anger.

Anger at something that hadn't even happened.

"She didn't do or say anything about my looks." She could feel her cheeks heat as someone passed them and she cleared her throat, patting Michael's lapel. "Why don't you tell me where you got up to? You were with Mr. Wilkens, right?"

It was a sufficient enough distraction for the time being. But it certainly would not be the last time she heard that rant. And it was easy to make the choice that night to steer very clear of Caroline, for both of their sakes.

December 19 – 2 Years Ago

The very last place Hannah wanted to be at was the Wilkens & Granger Christmas party.

Literally, she couldn't think of somewhere she wanted to be less than here. Eight years of these parties and she'd mostly figured out all of the steps. How to make the rounds, make conversation, without having to really think about it.

But the facts were these: she was a week away from Christmas. Her first Christmas without her mom. And every single day *hurt*. It just… hurt.

She would kill to be home with Abbie tonight.

"Do you have to look like it's killing you to be here?" Michael hissed into her ear as he pressed close enough for her to smell the cigar that he'd clearly smoked with the other law partners at the firm.

It was the numbness that had set in eight months ago that really done it. That made her snap into realizing – she simply did not care enough to put on the mask to please Michael. The mask had slowly been slipping in bits and pieces for the last five years or so, but this year… she went through the motions. She didn't have the extra energy to give him, anymore.

Hannah pulled her arm out of his grasp. "Would it kill you to pretend you give a damn about me being here?" She turned to face him. "You drag me here, make a point of showing me off, and then you disappear. What's the point of my presence at all beyond the first ten minutes?"

It was easy to say it here, easier than at home. She didn't bite her tongue the same way she used to, years ago, but she often tried to keep it as calm as possible for Abbie. But here, Michael would never scream. He would never throw items toward her or pound his fists into the walls next to her head, not in public.

The vein in his forehead pulsed as all of that anger flashed behind his eyes. "I don't even know what to *say* to you when you're like this." He leaned in only centimeters from her face, the hold he had around her wrist so tight, she knew it would leave the slightest mark. "You don't like it here? The life I've given you; *everything* I've given you? You'd have *nothing* without me, Hannah. Never forget that. And this? This is how we get it all. So, too fucking bad."

As he stormed away, she closed her eyes and leaned her head back against the wall, trying to just blend in with the background as best she could as she rubbed her wrist. It would be over soon.

She took stock of the room, as she breathed deeply. In and out. In an out, as she scanned her eyes over the people; it was the usual suspects. By this point in the evening, mostly everyone was a little tipsy. There was a lot of laughing, singing along to the music. Talking in the little groups. Hannah could pinpoint those groups easily now, she knew the people who would gravitate toward one another.

Her gaze landed on Caroline, so naturally. She stood in a suit – one of the many she owned.

Caroline Parker was always wearing suits… except at Fourth of July parties – her hand was on a woman's arm, as she threw her head back and laughed. It was genuine, boisterous laughter that reached Hannah from yards away.

It had been six years since she'd first met Caroline, but her face still drew Hannah like a bee to honey.

It was how she knew so much about her. Hannah had enough time at company events over the years that she'd made observations about most employees at Wilkens & Granger. But Caroline's face…

She couldn't help but watch her, the most.

Caroline was an outlier at these parties. She would mingle and talk to most of the groups for a while. Always polite and friendly, but never too close with anyone. If she came to office events alone – which was the most typical – she would put in a requisite amount of time, before ducking out politely.

Hannah envied that about her. She wondered if Caroline's dates appreciated it the way they should.

Because on occasion, she would bring a woman with her. No, not a woman, but women.

Different ones. Hannah didn't think she had ever seen the same one twice.

Regardless of whatever happened behind the scenes – maybe she was a player who went through women like nothing. But she wasn't married to them, so… good for her, Hannah supposed –

Caroline never left her dates for more than a minute or two. She brought them along to mingle with her. Her hand – she had long fingers, Hannah had noted – often rested along her date's lower back. But it was never a commanding touch; it always looked light, never forceful.

Like Caroline knew this was her domain and that her dates were here because of her, but like she truly appreciated that about them. She just looked like she was going to take care of things. That was the loudest impression Hannah had gotten from Caroline in the last six years.

Never demanding or angry or forceful, but a quiet power that exuded an air of "I have got this."

It must be nice, she thought for maybe the thousandth time, to feel that way. So in control. It was something else that added to Caroline's appeal. The appeal in observing her, anyway.

She watched that dimple appear next to Caroline's mouth as she grinned, listening attentively to something her date said. She wondered if Caroline's dates had any idea how lucky they were to have their dates' entire attention when they spoke, like their words were really being valued.

It just… must be nice.

It was the last thing she remembered focusing on before *it* happened.

It, being a man she didn't know coming into the room to announce that someone was having sex in the coat closet. She didn't know if he meant to announce it loudly or just to a group of people, but she was close enough to hear.

It, being the sinking feeling in her stomach as she took note that Michael wasn't in the room. And neither was Mindy, his secretary. With whom she knew he'd been having sex with for months.

It, being the uncontrollable reaction to walk, filled with a knowing dread, forward with the group of people. It felt as if she was watching herself in a daze, as the sounds of Michael and Mindy grew louder.

She couldn't bring herself to walk any further, as soon as she heard.

Hannah barely knew how she wound up on the twenty-first floor, sitting in the reception area of the empty floor where Michael used to work before he made partner. She didn't remember coming here. She just knew it was quiet and dark and she was alone.

She gripped her knees as she forced in deep breaths, and forced them out. This feeling inside of her, it wasn't heartbreak. No, Michael didn't have the power to cause that in her. She would have to love him for her heart to break, and it had been a long, long time since she'd ever even thought she might feel love for him.

She wasn't surprised by a long shot. She knew he'd been having an affair with Mindy, that she was just the latest in a long line. And, if she was being honest, that didn't really matter much, either, frankly. Other than her pride. Whatever was left of it, anyway.

But… just breathing hurt.

She had *nothing*.

She didn't have a mom anymore. She didn't have friends, other than Robyn, who Michael employed. She didn't have a job. No college degree. She had no real financial independence. Very little independence at all.

She didn't have a marriage in any of the ways it counted – passion, friendship, romance. She only had the public appearance of a marriage. And now? She didn't even have that.

She had humiliation and anger and helplessness and this deep feeling of emptiness that sat in the pit of her stomach.

Hannah forced in a deep breath, then forced it out.

She jumped when she felt something land gently on her lap and – when had anyone else come here?

She tensed, thinking it was Michael, but the soft, feminine scent didn't match, she realized seconds later, as her eyes focused on what actually was in her lap.

One of those little travel packs of tissues. She supposed it was meant for tears she didn't even feel.

Still, her hand shook as she moved to grip it in her fist, and she turned to look at –

Caroline.

She was slowly pulling her hand back from where she'd placed the tissues, clasping them in front of herself, as she tilted her head down to look Hannah in the eye.

It wasn't quite a smile on her lips, given the situation. But there was just a knowing look, something intended to be comforting, as Caroline spoke, "Sorry to invade your privacy. But I just had to get my jacket, from my office."

She gestured behind her, as if Hannah didn't know exactly where her office was. "And there are still some more in there if you need them. I left them on the desk. The door's unlocked."

Her voice was so quiet. It was soft, but it took up the silence. Like she would never have to yell to make herself heard, and she knew it. In this moment, Hannah held onto that strength, and she found herself staring up at Caroline, craving more of it.

She didn't think Caroline Parker would ever find herself in this sort of situation. And for some weird reason, the truth and strength of that made her feel just a little bit stronger herself.

"I also grabbed this for you at… the coat check," Caroline added and slipped Hannah's jacket from where it had been folded over her forearm. She hadn't even noticed it.

Hannah blinked in surprise as she took the jacket and settled it on her lap, still unable to find any words to speak aloud to process what was going on in her mind.

"I had to give your name at the door; didn't know if you'd want to go in there." Caroline tugged at her own jacket sleeve. Her tone was somehow both matter-of-fact and soothing, and Hannah could feel that combination settle over her.

Caroline didn't only give off the energy that said, *I'll take care of everything.* She truly did take care of things.

Hannah bunched her fingers around the material of her wool jacket, her throat tight, tongue-tied. Nothing. She had no words. Just, the nothingness resonating inside of her.

Caroline nodded.

She took a few steps toward the elevator, before she turned around again. The lights were still off on the floor, but Hannah thought there was a gentleness in Caroline's eyes. A softness that offset the sharp. It was such an odd thought to have in this moment, but then again, maybe it wasn't.

A perfect symmetry.

"You know, there are cabs out front, paid for by the firm. You just have to tell them you're here for Wilkens & Granger. And if you take the service entrance, you would likely avoid anyone from the party. If you need to go."

Hannah slowly nodded as she finally managed to find something, a tether within herself drawn out by Caroline, as she rasped out, "Thank you."

Caroline tilted her head in acknowledgement before she turned to get into the elevator.

Something about the finality of that head tilt, the way Caroline's voice had sounded in that last statement, blanketed over Hannah.

She, Hannah, could take care of things, too.

Her daughter. She had her daughter at home. That was what she did have. And Abbie was a big thing to have. A big enough reason to pull herself together.

She did take a cab. And the packet of tissues. If for no other reason than they reminded her of kindness, even if it felt like the world had shown her very little as of late.

By the time Michael came home, she was ready:

"I want a divorce." The words – the ones she'd thought for years, that had multiplied in strength through every affair, every fight, every time he'd threatened to take everything from her – scratched at her throat as they left, making her feel lighter for the first time in years.

He'd been shocked and initially tried to brush her off. Until he'd seen her packed suitcase by the door. Which was when the yelling had started, and he'd yelled… a lot. Some of it stuck in her mind, the way it had in the past when he'd said it: "Where do you fucking think you can go? You don't have anyone."

She knew that.

"If you walk out that door, I will take *everything* you care about that's left in this world, including Abbie, and you *know* I can."

Terrifyingly, yes, she knew that, too.

"You can't leave. Marriage is a contract, Hannah, and that contract lasts forever." They had been the least intimidating of his words, but the expensive cigar on his breath made her gag as her stomach had bottomed out. And with his words, he'd slammed his hands against her shoulders in a rare act of physicality, leaving her breathless as she hit the wall, and he slapped his hands on either side of her to cage her in.

But unlike every other time in the past when she'd wanted to leave, but moments like this, as the slither of terror moved through her… this time, she knew. This was it. This cage, this marriage, was over. She wasn't going to back down, not this time.

"There's no such thing as forever," she'd managed back through the distress that sat heavily in her nerves, grateful she'd brought Abbie to Robyn's for the night as soon as she'd returned home a few hours ago.

She was done.

January 5 – Last Year

"*I* wish you'd told me it was your birthday!" Robyn chastised as she sipped her coffee, leaning over the counter at The Bean Dream.

It was a slow evening – just after the post-work rush – and Robyn had come to drop Abbie off to her so she could hang out here while finishing the remainder of her shift. Just like the way Hannah used to do with her mom at the diner.

Hannah shook her head. "Don't be silly; I've really gotten all I could need today."

Hannah had long since stopped expecting anything on her birthday. Especially in the last two years, after her mom died and everything was shit with Michael.

Abbie had run up to her and given her a big grin as she'd handed Hannah a card she'd made for her in art class that day. The tight hug she'd gotten from her daughter was really the best gift she could have gotten.

Well, that and the text she'd received from Caroline earlier that confirmed their next meeting.

Their first official meeting, since she'd grinned at Hannah at the end of their lunch and said, "Though you are my client, I like to keep things a little more official than Sunday lunch. So, I'll draw up some contracts later this week and we'll officially get started?"

It was so odd, she'd realized at that moment. Well, the entirety of lunch had felt odd, really.

It was odd how she'd known Caroline, peripherally, for the better part of a decade, but how she didn't truly know her at all. It was odd how Caroline's face was all perfect angles and somehow stayed both sharp and went soft when she smiled. It was odd how Hannah realized that she didn't think she'd truly been on the receiving end of that smile – not the *real* one – despite their handfuls of interactions.

It was definitely odd how Caroline had thought they were on a date. God, her cheeks still burned in embarrassment at that. Definitely her own stupid fault! Writing her number on a coffee cup; she worked at a café! She should have known how that would be perceived!

Hannah glanced at Abbie, who was reading and sipping at a hot chocolate at the table she'd claimed as her favorite near the window. She felt so bad about the number of times in the last year that Abbie had to spend hours at the café with her, but…

Well, she tried to remind herself of the many hours she'd spent at Jimmy's Diner with her mother. She'd loved it there, for the most part. When she'd been younger, for sure.

"About that," Robyn's voice pulled her out of her thoughts. "I don't mean to burst any of your bubbles, but… how do you really know you can trust that woman?"

"She's my only option." The truth came out quickly, even with Robyn's doubtful look.

"Look, I am not trying to be a downer, because you know I'm so glad you are getting things rolling with the divorce, legally. But this Caroline woman, she knows Michael. You said they worked together, right? I just… I'm a little wary is all. The guy my sister worked with when she got divorced was really good, I could get you the number–"

"No. It has to be Caroline." Hannah was resolute as she interrupted Robyn.

She didn't mean to be rude; Robyn had made the offer for her sister's lawyer a few times in the last year and was just trying to help.

But what Hannah had come to learn after tossing and turning over this for months, was that it *had* to be Caroline Parker.

Caroline was the only lawyer that got under Michael's skin, she was the only one that had ever made Michael question himself. The only one he'd ever ranted about losing cases to. The one person he fixated on at work. Which made Hannah know that Caroline was damn good at her job.

And for the many things Michael was terrible at – being a father and a husband top of the list – being a lawyer was unfortunately not one of them.

She needed someone great.

And she needed someone who was not friendly with Michael and would be willing to go against him, despite his connections and power and money.

The truth was that the list of people she trusted was very, very short.

Robyn… well, that might really be it. She didn't have any family, and it made her feel that ugly kind of embarrassed and ashamed that she hated looking at in the mirror when she thought about the friendships she'd given up or let fade over the years out of Michael's insistence.

So, did she know that she could really trust Caroline? Did she really trust her? She barely knew the woman.

Both she and Robyn looked down in surprise when her phone buzzed on the counter between them.

"Did she plant a bug on you?" Robyn asked, and Hannah could tell she was only half joking.

Caroline Parker - 6:17PM
Aside from death of a loved one, divorce is the biggest stressor in an adult's life. Now that you are officially my client, I just want to check in with you and tell you that I'm here. It's my job to make it less stressful.

So take a deep breath, welcome to the Caroline Parker Team, and remind yourself: You got this.

Hannah blinked down at the message, a confused swirling of feelings running through her stomach.

She knew Caroline *seemed* genuine. She always had.

But Hannah had been duped before by someone that she'd thought was genuine. She'd misjudged character so much that she'd married the worst person she'd ever met.

So, the truth was? The person she trusted the least in her life in a lot of ways, was herself.

Still. Caroline didn't *have* to send this message in what appeared to be a sweet gesture to a new client experiencing a tough time. She didn't *have* to agree to work with Hannah pro bono. She didn't *have* to bring Hannah her jacket or tissues that night Michael had been caught cheating.

It had been the tissues that did it for her.

It had been the tissues, that small package of tissues that Hannah still had yet to get rid of, that convinced her to find Caroline's new number after she'd switched firms, months ago.

Because Caroline didn't have to show her a kindness that night. A kindness that no one else had shown her, even people who had pretended to be friendly with her for years.

Hannah shook her head slowly as her phone screen darkened, and she looked up at Robyn. "I have to take the chance."

April 22 – Last Year

"All right! I'm off to save the world with this Abbacado," Caroline informed them as she stretched.

She wrapped an arm around Abbie's shoulders, before she stroked her hand over Hannah's shoulder.

It was Earth Day, and Caroline's environmentally-friendly firm was having a big cleanup along the river to promote an anti-littering campaign. Abbie had been so excited to take part, and Hannah would have, too, if she wasn't working shortly.

Caroline had dropped by her place to pick up Abbie for the afternoon ten minutes ago, where she'd paused to chat with Hannah and Robyn.

She looked up from where she sat at the kitchen table, still with Robyn. "Thanks so much for taking her; she's been talking about it all week."

Really, Abbie talked about Caroline all of the time, all days, all weeks.

Caroline was already smiling down at her. "Well, good. So have I."

"You have?" Abbie asked, zipping up her jacket in the doorway.

Caroline turned to face her. "Been telling everyone I know about it, obviously."

Abbie beamed at her.

Caroline turned to face her again. "You just come by when you're done at the café? We'll be back at mine by then." Hannah nodded, and Caroline gave Robyn a smaller, more polite smile. "It was really nice to meet you."

Robyn waited only until the door was closed behind them before she stared Hannah down and asked, "You know that woman is in love with you, right?"

Hannah gaped in surprise at the comment, her cheeks feeling uncontrollably warm as she quickly denied, "No, she isn't."

Robyn shot her with a knowing look. "Hannah, I just think you need to be a little careful is all. You are taking a major chance trusting her with everything and I think you're walking a fine line. That's all." She held her hands up as if to say she'd said her piece.

Hannah just shook her head, her stomach twisting for a lot of reasons – but, no. Caroline could have any woman she wanted. She didn't want a mess like Hannah. Thankfully, or this could get really messy, given how much she'd tossed into this chance in the last few months.

No. Definitely not.

June 20 – Last Year

The chance paid off. It really did.

It didn't fully hit her until the summer solstice, two full weeks after the divorce had been finalized.

"Mom! Look!" Abbie shouted as she rollerbladed by her – a little wobbly still, but getting so much better by the minute.

Hannah put her hand up to shield her gaze from the sun as she lounged in the park near Abbie's school. Yesterday had been the official last day, and today the school was hosting a big cookout party for all of the future fifth-graders.

"You're doing so great, honey!"

Abbie's friends in her class had been particularly excited for the rollerskating area of the park, therefore, Abbie was rearing to try it as well. Though, she'd never been particularly into skating before, so Hannah was decently sure it wasn't something her daughter was going to obsess over.

Still, she was giggling so brightly, so loudly, having such a good time, that Hannah couldn't help but smile as she reclined against the picnic table at her back. She'd been more than happy to agree to sit down here and keep an eye on the girls.

"Mom, you gotta come and skate, too!" Abbie shouted, a little out of breath as she skated quickly by her.

Hannah arched her eyebrows and shook her head as she laughed.

"Yeah, you gotta come and skate," she heard the joking voice from behind her, and she whipped her head around to see Caroline approaching.

Her face shifted into a big, easy smile automatically, excited for the company even as she was surprised. "Hey! What are you doing here?"

"Caroline! You came!" Abbie shouted from across the paved area she was skating on. She pushed her helmet up over her now extremely messy hair and waved at her best friend with abject excitement written all over her face.

"Aaand Abbie invited you. Of course," she sighed, but it was affection she felt.

It scared her, sometimes, just how attached Abbie had become to Caroline in such a short time. If only because there was the possibility of anything happening and Caroline walking away from them. She wasn't obligated to be with them in any way, especially now that they'd finalized the divorce.

Caroline was no longer her lawyer. She was a presence in her life; in their lives.

And if Hannah was honest with herself, the night before her final hearing for the divorce, she'd been riddled with anxiety. The anxiety had kept her awake all night – revolving around what would happen regarding Abbie's custody, mostly. And a thousand other things involving Abbie and Michael and money and, and, and…

But then a thought that stopped her dead in her tracks – at the height of her anxieties, after Abbie – was… would Caroline leave them, now?

The thought had made a cold stone of dread sink in her stomach. Because Abbie had gotten so attached; she idolized Caroline. And it was such a pure love that Hannah adored seeing it on her daughter's face. She didn't know what she'd do if Caroline decided that it was over, when the divorce was over.

They were friends; Caroline wasn't watching Abbie and hanging out with her out of the fact that she was the world's greatest divorce attorney. No, she knew that. But the what ifs ran her ragged.

But here Caroline was. Two weeks post-divorce and showing up as usual.

"She invites me, and I come running." Caroline bowed as if to royalty, before straightening and smiling at Hannah.

There was something about Caroline's smile that she found so gripping.

"She does have that power," she agreed.

She took in Caroline's casual attire – she'd seen her out of business suits in the last six months many times. But in a way, it was still so odd, given that it was almost all she'd ever seen her in for the eight years they'd known one another before this – the leggings and the button-up shirt that had a little tie on the side.

Her clothing always showed off the curves in her body and always spoke of quiet expense. Never flashy, the way Michael was with his money. Caroline had subtly classy taste, and she'd never once made Hannah feel less than in any way.

Then again, now that she knew Caroline's family and that she'd come from a background similar to Hannah's own… it made sense.

"Well, here's the rub – your genius child is right. We can't sit here and not skate at all," Caroline said as she sat on the bench next to Hannah.

She turned to look at Caroline, arching a dubious eyebrow at her. "Excuse me?"

Caroline laughed and slid Hannah a pair of rollerblades. "Got your size and mine from the little rental stand."

She meant to say no. She opened her mouth to say no.

But she heard Abbie cheering her on, and Caroline was smiling that smile at her – so cajoling and soft and engaging, with her wavy hair half-tied back and her dark eyes glinting brightly…

Ten minutes later, she'd let go of some of her tentative feelings on the skates and moved a little faster…

"You put up all of this resistance and you're good at this?!" Caroline exclaimed next to her.

Hannah shook her head, casting her eyes toward the ground. "I'm not good at this, I haven't done it in years. I just *used* to be good at it." She glimpsed at Caroline, who skated easily alongside her. "You, though, appear to be actually good at this."

Caroline shrugged. "Also more of a muscle memory. I have three older brothers! My childhood was all about catching up to them."

Hannah opened her mouth to retort, before she instead gasped as her wheel hit a stick – a freaking stick could take her down! She dimly recalled that being a reason she hadn't loved skating as she'd aged – and she flailed her arms out, sliding one foot forward on the rollerblade, as the other remained wedged and she was going down –

Until she found herself caught in Caroline's arms.

Caroline had downplayed her skills for certain, Hannah thought, because she was sturdy as she held up Hannah and gently got her back to a balanced stand. "You okay?" She whispered, but kept her arms around Hannah's midsection just in case.

Hannah nodded, her heart still beating like crazy in her chest even though she knew she was in no danger of falling now. And still, she kept her arms where they were over Caroline's shoulders.

It was a warm day, and the warmth of Caroline's body was only inches away from being pressed against her. But it didn't make her feel too hot, feel the need to move away.

Instead… she felt safe.

It was so odd. So silly, really, because even if she had fallen, she would have been absolutely fine.

But, as she gazed down at Caroline, who was looking up at her with an indecipherable look on her face, she realized that this safety wasn't just about this fall.

"I got you, don't worry," Caroline murmured, giving her a little smile with just the edge of her lips. "Just take a second."

It was in that moment, with the sun beaming down brightly, her daughter laughing, and knowing that she had nothing hanging over her head, that she truly realized how free she'd felt.

And in this exact moment, how utterly protected.

And both feelings came at the hands of the woman giving her a small, inquisitive smile.

She was free from Michael, she'd walked away knowing Abbie had her best interests all taken care of, she was getting her own life back and… it was all good.

She was lucky Caroline hadn't walked away after the divorce, and not just because Abbie loved her, she acknowledged for the first time. But because she'd come to love Caroline, too. She was the best friend she'd ever had.

"You good?" Caroline asked.

Hannah nodded after a long moment, before shaking her head at herself and releasing Caroline from her hold. "I – sorry, yeah. Got a little lost in my own thoughts."

Caroline gave her a curious look, because she was far from an idiot, but didn't ask. She rarely asked, and Hannah appreciated that a lot.

She let her arms drop quickly, before giving Caroline a self-deprecating look. "You're always saving me."

She shook her head as the words came out; she'd intended them to be playful, but… they rang so true. So true that it almost upset her; if she wasn't careful enough, she'd rely far too much on Caroline.

She sometimes feared she already did.

"Oof," Caroline grunted as Abbie skated right into her side.

"Come play with us?" Abbie asked, tilting her head up at Caroline.

Who gave Hannah an apologetic smile. "Duty calls… you good?" She asked again.

Hannah nodded and smiled warmly. "I am good."

She was.

Her life, thanks to Caroline, was very, very good. And she wasn't going to let herself get too bogged down in that, not today.

August 9 – Last Year

Hannah had spent her daughter's entire birthday party in a fog. The same fog she'd been living in since one o'clock in the morning.

Since that moment, time had seemed to stop and be stamped in her mind. Since the moment she'd come so close to being kissed for the first time in years.

By Caroline.

She hadn't quite known how they'd gotten to that point in the night, that led Caroline to leaning into her, lips hovering just over Hannah's own. So close, it had shocked her and she'd moved to push Caroline away by taking a fistful of her camisole, but –

Then Abbie had come running in, thankfully. Because if Caroline had kissed her or if she'd pushed her away first, it could have been disastrous for them.

But she knew that she'd have regretted it big time. She'd felt terrible all night, needing to apologize and move on.

Everything should be okay, she thought, since Caroline had come to the party and they'd apologized and said things could be normal. But it had only been a couple of hours and she could already feel that things were not normal.

Caroline didn't stand close to her, not like she normally did. Not at all through the party. Not once.

Hannah didn't know how to deal with that, because on one hand she was grateful for the space but on the other... she was already so confused and she didn't want things to change. She desperately did not want more things to change in her life.

Caroline approached her for the first time since she'd arrived with her hands tucked into her pockets, at the end of the evening, and had given Hannah a little smile. "Hey. I just wanted to come and say goodbye."

"Goodbye?" She'd asked. "The party's still going."

Caroline nodded slowly, shoulders shrugging up to her ears as she kicked her sneakered foot at the grass. "Yeah, but I have an early breakfast meeting with a client tomorrow that I still have to prep for, and... you know. Takes time."

Hannah had been married to someone who'd lied to her face for nearly a decade. She could spot a lie from a mile away, from someone who was much better at it than Caroline.

Caroline had become the person who was the first to arrive in Hannah's life and the last to leave.

She wasn't the person who left early for flimsy excuses.

But she couldn't push it, because what could she say?

She wanted things to be normal between them. And if Caroline felt embarrassed about what had happened the night before and needed some more time to get back to their baseline, then Hannah could grin and bear it.

"Right," Hannah said softly, brushing her hair back from her face. "I'll see you Tuesday?"

She held her breath for that moment, crossing every finger and toe before Caroline smiled. A small one, not her full, big, confident one. But a smile nonetheless. "Of course."

She breathed out a sigh of relief, because at least she could count on that. Caroline wouldn't break her word, she was sure of it.

Still, it was stilted and weird and she felt off about it for the rest of the afternoon.

There was something inside of her that she couldn't quite... put a finger on. About this whole thing. About everything, and... ugh.

She flung her arm over her eyes as she laid in bed late that night, thankful that Abbie and her friends' giggles and whispers and squeals had slowly quieted into sleep by now. She needed time with her thoughts.

"You know that woman is in love with you, right?" Robyn's words rang in her ears.

She'd laughed Robyn off then and had continued to do so for months afterwards. Caroline could have any woman she wanted! Hannah was positive of that. Caroline was absolutely gorgeous, she was incredibly intelligent, she was capable, she was the most thoughtful person in the world.

What would she want with Hannah?

But Caroline had leaned in to kiss her last night. She'd initiated that whole moment.

Hannah frowned, then, eyes snapping open as she stared up at her ceiling, the fog in her brain shifting ever so slightly. *Had* Caroline initiated it?

She squinted, thinking back to the night before.

Caroline had stopped over to help bake. She'd put the cupcakes in the oven... and she'd turned to face Hannah, wearing only her thin camisole after she'd shed her suit jacket upon arrival. It had been so hot baking for hours and hours in August.

They'd been drinking – not enough to be drunk, but enough to let go. She'd apparently surprised Caroline by telling her about Abbie's hero worship, which seemed insane to her. How did Caroline not know?

"Must get annoying, hearing about me all of the time," Caroline had teased. "Caroline's so amazing, Caroline needs a superhero cape, Caroline is just so good at everything."

Hannah had laughed quietly, reveling in this feeling they'd built between them over the last eight months. Where they'd moved from client-attorney to friends to best friends. It was the closest she'd ever felt to another human being, if she was honest with herself. It felt foolish, almost, saying that at her age after having been *married* for over a decade, but it was all true.

She'd skimmed her eyes down Caroline's clavicle over the three freckles she had on her chest – huh. When had she memorized those? – and it just amused her.

To see Caroline covered in the chocolate cupcake batter was amusing to her because Caroline… she really did seem to be good at just about everything else. But when it came to baking, she never quite hit the mark, and she made a total mess doing it.

It was rather endearing.

She didn't know why, she had only known that she had to trace her fingers over it. Over the batter, tracing her fingertips over the mess Caroline had made of herself. She'd only been mixing the batter! How… Hannah had shaken her head, fondly tracing the long line of chocolate that Caroline had apparently whipped right out of the bowl and onto herself.

It looked good enough to eat.

The – the batter did.

"How did you even do this?" She'd tilted her head down at Caroline, breathing in the same warm air in the room.

Caroline had cleared her throat before speaking, "I guess my baking ability is one thing you will never have to hear Abbie loving about me. It's just everything else you'll have to be annoyed at."

Hannah had stared at Caroline, hearing the self-deprecating tone. She knew Caroline had meant it as a joke, but she also knew Caroline, and she knew that there was more behind it. She knew that Caroline felt badly that Abbie idolized her so much instead of Hannah herself, and the thing was… it might have bothered Hannah if it was anyone else, too.

It was how the endeared, affectionate smile took over her face as she'd stroked the skin under her hand on Caroline's chest. "It would be annoying, if I didn't agree with everything she says about you."

Caroline had scoffed and shaken her head, and she knew Caroline was going to rebuff her words.

There had been a strong, urgent need for Caroline to just – for her to understand where Hannah was coming from. That she meant everything she said. For her to know how vital she was, instead of working to the bone for everyone around her and always downplaying it.

She'd flattened her hand against Caroline's chest, and she'd never touched her there, before. She didn't know why it registered so strongly in her brain, but it had. She knew she'd never touched Caroline here, never felt how soft the skin of her chest was. Never felt how warm she was, right above her big heart. Felt how that heart raced, right against the palm of her hand.

She felt Caroline's breath stutter out against her face as she'd insisted, "If I could have my daughter look up to anyone in our lives, I would choose you. And you aren't allowed to brush this off."

And in that moment, as Caroline had looked up at her with wide, uncertain eyes, she needed her to see how important she was.

Because at this stage of her life, she meant… she'd meant that she *wanted* Abbie to look up to Caroline even more than having Abbie look up to herself. Because Hannah – well, she knew she'd had her reasons for staying with Michael for so long, but it didn't help her sleep at night.

She was doing better, now, but she'd been angry at herself for a long time. Hannah regretted so many of her choices, and she'd lived in those regrets even after they compounded upon themselves.

Caroline, she was different.

She pressed her hand more firmly against Caroline's chest, feeling the vitality in the heartbeat under her fingers. "You are strong and smart and gorgeous and good."

She'd stroked her fingers over the skin there, just feeling the meaning of those words settle inside of her own chest. Because she had meant them, every single one in equal measure.

Caroline was those things. She was strong enough to fight all of her own battles and shoulder so many others. To help Hannah, to be there for Abbie, to be the one her parents relied on the most whenever they struggled. For all of the rest of her clients like Hannah, the ones who needed her.

She was smart enough to handle it all and do it with grace.

She was so, so gorgeous, with all of the different smiles she had. Hannah knew all of those smiles by now, and each one had a shade of meaning.

And most of all, she was so good. Her goodness was in every action, every moment.

She was so much more than Hannah could have ever fathomed before really knowing her. She was so much more than she gave herself credit for. She was just so much *more*, Hannah thought, as she looked down into wide, brown eyes, as she felt Caroline's heartbeat staccato under her hand.

This was Caroline. Who had cut Michael off at the knees, who worked into late hours in the night and shifted around her schedule to help not just Hannah and Abbie, but everyone else.

This was Caroline, whose sheer strength and will and composure had inspired Hannah herself to keep on going in her own life. To keep picking up the pieces she'd been missing and really put herself together.

This was Caroline, who was brilliant and sweet and beautiful inside and out, and…

"You're kind of my hero, too," she whispered, not even realizing the words snuck out of her throat.

Hannah hadn't realized she'd closed her eyes again as she thought over the night's events, but they snapped open again as she sat up sharply in bed, her own heart racing.

No, no it hadn't been Caroline at all who had initiated it. Not really. Maybe she'd leaned in, but… but it had been Hannah herself all along.

Telling Caroline how beautiful she was? Saying she was Hannah's own personal hero?!

She hadn't even realized that her hand had been so close to Caroline's chest, her fingers touching the tops of her breasts until this moment, and she could still feel the sensation on her fingers like a phantom. She could still taste her breath, feel the way her full lips had been just a whisper away from Hannah's own.

She stood from her bed quickly, unable to lay so still when it felt like her world was spinning, her blood rushing.

So, yes, she'd thought Caroline was beautiful, gorgeous, stunning. She always had, from the first moment she'd seen her. But – but the thoughts *had* been more present lately.

It was the itch at the back of her neck combined with the tugging low in her stomach, that had her falling to her knees to pull her sketchpad out from under her bed where she'd slid it the night before last night, and she opened it with shaking hands.

And as she flipped through it, her breath was stolen right from her lungs so quickly it made her dizzy.

It was all right here, she thought dimly, as she flipped through the book.

Caroline. Day after day and – and not in any sort of normal way.

She froze as she looked down at her own drawing, something she'd created by her own hand, and…

How had she not realized it?

Tentatively, she brought a hand down to trace over the little dimple in Caroline's cheek that she'd shaded in on her drawing from Father's Day. She was radiant. And she was everywhere.

"Oh, god," Hannah muttered to herself, shaking her head as she sat back on her haunches and stared sightlessly across the room.

It felt like everything slotted into place in that moment, like her brain had been missing a key piece to understanding herself in the last few months and it finally clicked into place.

Oh, god.

But – but she was nowhere near ready for that. She was nowhere near ready to be with anyone else, and certainly not Caroline.

No.

Hannah closed her eyes tightly and flipped her sketchpad shut with finality. Not happening; she was going to shut this down right here and now.

October 19 – Last Year

The thing was, it was far, far more difficult than Hannah ever thought it would be to shut down her feelings for Caroline.

She tried not to blame herself too much – the only significant romantic relationship in her life had been with Michael. And she hadn't really had to shut down those feelings; no, they had crashed and burned a slow, agonizing death with all of his indiscretions, lies, and intimidations over the years.

And she'd never *fallen* before for anyone else. Hadn't had any opportunity or interest in doing so, given how wrapped up her life had been in her marriage, for better or worse… mostly worse.

But how the hell was she supposed to shut down her feelings for Caroline?! She was desperate to know.

"Mom! Keep up!" Abbie called over her shoulder about twenty feet ahead of Hannah, giddy as she walked through the pumpkin patch.

Caroline walked alongside her daughter, as Hannah had encouraged when they'd arrived to pick their pumpkins.

"You two don't have to wait for me," she'd urged them as she'd taken her time getting out of the car; it had been a plan for her own self-preservation. The less time spent alone in any fashion with Caroline since the previous weekend, the weekend where they'd shared a bed at Hangout Weekend, the better.

Caroline hadn't questioned her, other than a quick look that flitted over her features. That also had happened a few times since last weekend.

Abbie, however, *had* questioned her, as she'd shaken her head dramatically. "You and Caroline should walk together, Mom. What if you trip and fall on a vine! Who's gonna catch you?"

Both she and Caroline had given her daughter perplexed looks at that. Abbie had given a guileless look and shrugged, "It happens in movies."

"What the heck kind of movies are you watching?" Caroline had asked, bumping her hip into Abbie with a laugh, throwing a joking glance back at Hannah.

She'd returned it with a smile of her own, before shaking her head. "I'm going to grab the cart for us; you two are the ones who actually want to carve the pumpkins, so… go on."

She needed to spend less time close to Caroline, because… Because! Just thinking about it made her flustered!

It should have worked, keeping a lagging distance between them.

Except for the fact that her eyes continued to fall to the curve of Caroline's ass in her high-waisted light-wash jeans. She had an amber sweater tucked into them and, and her butt just looked obscenely *good* in them.

She'd done that far too much lately. Hannah's cheeks heated even as she breathed out an exasperated sigh at herself. She'd never been this person, before.

She didn't even recognize the person she was when she was wrapped up in wanting Caroline, because nothing had ever been like this for her in her life.

She'd, embarrassingly, asked Karla – her new friend in several of her architecture classes – about how to sort out her feelings as they'd had coffee during a class break once. "I feel…" She rolled her lips, searching for the words, before admitting, "*Ridiculous* asking you about this. But other than Caroline, I don't really have any friends who are…"

"Queer," Karla filled in with a knowing nod. She was grinning though, as she'd waved her hand and encouraged, "Hit me with the gay dilemma."

So she had. About everything.

About how she'd known Caroline for years, but had only really seen into her soul for the last ten months, but it had been the most enlightening ten months. About everything Caroline did for her, for Abbie, everything she meant for them.

Karla had nodded slowly. "I mean – first, she sounds perfect. Where do I get one?" She laughed at herself as she took a sip of her latte, and added, "Are you sure – and I don't mean for this to sound the wrong way – you're sure that it's truly about you having feelings for Caroline? Like, attraction, wanting, all-encompassing feelings, and not just, uh, that she is so amazing and is also a lesbian and you have some wires crossed? Because that could be terrible."

And Hannah had sat with that, she really had.

Only...

Only, Caroline had then informed her that she was going on a date. And Hannah had felt – she didn't know how to explain that feeling that dropped through her in actual words. Angry, only she had no reason to be angry. No one to be angry at. Caroline wasn't Michael. Caroline wasn't married to her, wasn't obligated to her as anything more than her friend.

And at the root of her anger was sheer jealousy.

It ate through everything inside of her, settling in a big, heavy, ugly tangle that threatened to make her sick in the pit of her stomach. Every time she thought about it. About who this other woman was? About what Caroline wore on her date? About – would Caroline look at this woman the way she looked at Hannah?

Would this woman deserve Caroline?

Did *she*?

By the time that jealousy was under control... well, last weekend had happened.

Last weekend, where she'd learned that Caroline had had sex with her friend Jess, several years ago.

Hannah had been floating – the only time she'd been drunk in any way in many years, and she'd felt safe and content and happy.

Until Jess had commented that Caroline was *definitely up in her top three lovers*.

Hannah had choked on her drink, eyes snapping open to stare at Caroline and Jess, where they'd been leaning against one another on the floor. So comfortable.

It had been a monster, that time, even more untamable than the last.

Because these two were right in front of her eyes. This woman, Caroline's friend, was right there. Joking and laughing and touching Caroline, and *they'd had sex*.

Hannah – she'd never felt that reaction. And she'd been married to someone who had sex outside of their marriage. Often.

It had certainly been an eye-opener for her. Let alone what had happened that night in bed.

Where her guard had been so far down, she'd pursued questioning Caroline about sex. Until she'd gotten so wet, she'd had to sneak into the bathroom and touch herself or she might have come in that bed from Caroline's voice alone.

And this all brought her back to now.

As she watched Caroline bend down to look over a pumpkin, and those jeans stretched so well over her ass, which was so full and Hannah wanted to…

She slapped a hand over her eyes. What was wrong with her?! She'd never once been this person! She'd never been someone who couldn't keep her eyes and thoughts appropriate!

She'd never lusted like this, never wanted like this.

She never –

"Hey, you okay?" Caroline asked, her voice right next to Hannah's ear.

She jumped, feeling that warm breath washing over her, down her neck, and sending that hot feeling spiraling through her body. The one she'd only ever experienced from Caroline.

She startled, sliding her hand from her eyes over her racing heart. "Oh! I, uh…" She opened and closed her mouth a couple of times, before shaking her head. Then nodding. "Yes, I'm okay. Just, I just have a little bit of a headache."

"You want to head home? We can just grab the first good looking pumpkins we see and leave?" Caroline offered, with that concerned look in her eyes. So, so sweet.

The attraction she felt for Caroline was unparalleled. The feelings she kept a tight lid on as best she could grew stronger every single day, and whenever Caroline gave her this kind of look – spoiler? She did so, often – the very fibers of Hannah's being begged her to give in. They railed against her self-control when it came to Caroline, asking her *why not?*

She gave Caroline a smile and shook her head again, all too aware of how close they were as she shifted back and forth on her feet. She'd been very conscientious to not touch in the last week, for very obvious reasons.

"No, no it's okay. I'm okay."

The look Caroline gave her was all too knowingly doubtful, but she reluctantly acquiesced as Abbie shouted from a bit in the distance, "Caroline! This one is the biggest! Let's get it!"

"Soooo demanding!" Caroline shouted over her shoulder toward Abbie playfully, winking at Hannah.

She managed a weak smile in response as Caroline turned to march over to Abbie and very seriously inspect the pumpkin together.

And she watched them, answering those thoughts.

That is why not. That right there… was why not.

Because Caroline? She was the forever kind of woman; it was what she was looking for, by her very own admission in several conversations, and Hannah just didn't believe in forevers, anymore.

And even if she could get over that to give it a go – she heard Abbie's loud giggle at the way Caroline grabbed her with mock-desperation and lightly shook her shoulders, commanding that she treat the pumpkins with respect – she wasn't the only one who would get hurt when it went wrong.

November 12 – Last Year

Hannah didn't quite know what possessed her to say it on Caroline's birthday. To say her mother's sacred birthday ritual to her – "Anything you want, within my power, is yours," Betty would say.

Hannah didn't even do it on Abbie's birthday. She didn't know why; perhaps it was because her daughter generally got whatever she wanted on her birthday, in a much more traditional birthday setting? Abbie didn't have to make a particular wish the way Hannah had in her youth, because she got to go on real vacations and take day trips and have all of the experiences Hannah wished for her.

But as she watched Caroline slip into her jacket as she was leaving on the night of her birthday, Hannah felt... swept up in it all.

Swept up in Caroline, when she didn't even do anything. Nothing out of the ordinary for her, anyway.

Caroline gave herself to everyone and got so little in return. Sure, Hannah made her dinner. And the cookies she remembered Caroline enjoying from the first time they'd met – that... well, that was a whole other thing.

But it wasn't enough.

And here was Caroline, smiling and telling Hannah that she had a good time. Smiling with her face – her perfect, perfect face – healing from all the bruising and the small cuts, with her wrist still in a brace, and every single time Hannah had seen Caroline for the last two weeks had been so painful.

Seeing Caroline hurt like that on Halloween, it had broken something down in Hannah. That was where it all started. Her resolve had been so strong, but it had started breaking down when she'd walked into Caroline's apartment and wanted nothing more than to tear apart the man who'd hurt her while taking care of Caroline at the same time.

It was an urge unlike anything she'd ever felt in her life, and in the weeks since, Hannah often felt like she was powerless to stop herself from getting even closer. No matter how bad the consequences would be.

And she felt it again, now. The desperate want to be so close to Caroline, as she offered, "Whatever you want, within my power, is yours."

She echoed her mom's words to the woman in front of her, but she felt such a different meaning with them. She wanted to give Caroline the world. But if all that could mean right now was something small Caroline asked for… then, so be it.

Caroline looked at her intently for a long moment, dark eyes searching hers as she let out a sigh.

A sigh that Hannah couldn't give a name to, but it made something leap inside of her. Something *wanting*.

That happened far, far too much.

But then Caroline dropped her gaze and went to play with the zipper of her jacket as she answered, "I'll have to think–"

Hannah was already nodding – of course she'd have to think about it – when Caroline paused and tilted her head. "What about the answer to a question?"

Hannah arched her eyebrows, incredulous. But, this was Caroline. Caroline *would* want something like the answer to a question. Still… "A question?"

She'd answer whatever question she could for Caroline, but honestly, she wasn't sure there was much she knew that Caroline didn't.

The glint in Caroline's eyes made Hannah swallow hard as soon as it was trained on her. This was lawyer Caroline, now. This was Caroline with her teeth dug into a topic. This was the Caroline who represented her in her divorce. A Caroline who was laser-focused, smelled blood in the water, and knew what to say to get information she needed to hear.

This Caroline frightened Hannah almost as much as she found her ridiculously, utterly sexy.

Her stomach clenched.

"On Halloween, you said that my not showing up to Abbie's party was what you were afraid of and that as soon as I knew… but you didn't finish."

Oh. Oh no.

Hannah's stomach dropped out with an entirely different feeling. Dread. Oh, no.

She had said that. She'd felt so certain that Caroline must have known, after the lake house, that Hannah wanted her *so* badly. That once Caroline knew how much Hannah wanted her, that it would all come crashing down, this friendship. This… this special relationship.

She could feel the color leave her cheeks as her anxiety ratcheted up, and she started toying with her fingers nervously, trying to think. Trying to think of anything to say, of how to navigate this.

But of course, as usual when she felt pressure or high emotion, she felt tongue-tied. And with her lack of anything to say other than, "I was terrified that as soon as you knew how you light my body and feelings on fire, you would start acting differently, and I want you to want me back, but it's what I'm most afraid of, too!"

She could feel her cheeks heat with the words unsaid, and she diverted her gaze to the coat rack behind Caroline as she bit the side of her tongue to try to think.

Caroline cleared her throat, shaking back her hair as she looked a little embarrassed. "I mean, maybe it's silly, but I…"

Oh no, she thought again as Caroline cut herself off and then leaned in. Leaned in just enough to catch Hannah's gaze and make her feel powerless to look away, even as her heart thudded in her chest.

"What is it that you think I know? What are you afraid of?" Caroline's voice was soft but determined. It was a voice that not only demanded answers but made you want to give them.

God, Caroline was so good at what she did.

"Nothing," she managed to say. The lie made her nerves tangle even tighter. "It was just– I was angry and my mind was going in a hundred different directions and that just slipped out."

She couldn't even convince herself with those words, and she knew she didn't convince Caroline, either. Hannah dropped her gaze again, feeling herself tense even tighter, like a volcano ready to explode. She couldn't look Caroline in the eye while she lied to her like that.

With Michael, she could do it in an instant. The same way he did to her. But she couldn't do it, now. Not with her.

Caroline sought out her eyes again, and they alone begged the truth even without words. She ducked her head and moved closer, close enough now that Hannah felt surrounded by her light, clean scent. It was something she'd come to associate with comfort over the last eleven months, but she couldn't take comfort right now.

"It's obviously not nothing," Caroline murmured, her voice so quiet but somehow so loud as she called out Hannah's untruths.

She couldn't – she couldn't – she had to meet Caroline's gaze as the desperation inside of her started to peek out. "Please don't push this. You… you know," her voice was low, absolutely pleading, but she didn't care.

She didn't know how to do this. She didn't know how to have a relationship with Caroline. She didn't know how to really have a relationship at all right now.

It was just made so much more complicated by how much she wanted one.

"I just want it to stay in the box it's in because as soon as we talk about it, as soon as the box is open, it'll be different."

Everything would be. As soon as Caroline acknowledged that she could have Hannah – that Hannah wanted her. That Hannah had never felt more desire than when she thought of Caroline. That Hannah laid in bed during their nightly phone calls and felt that the world was at peace, like she could actually sleep restfully for the first time in forever. That Hannah had never slept as well as she did when Caroline had laid on top of her and snuggled in close –

It was all over.

This tender, steady, stable, dependable relationship they'd cultivated would be gone.

Caroline tossed her hands in the air, exasperation apparent. "What will be different? What do you think I know because I have no idea what you're talking about!"

She sounded so genuine, but how! Hannah couldn't fathom it, she truly couldn't. She'd laid in bed next to Caroline, staring at her when she'd been drunk because she'd been unable to keep her eyes off of her gorgeous body, and had Caroline fuck her.

Maybe not really. Not physically.

But in her mind, that had been exactly what had happened. That's what it felt like. Hannah's memories were blurry but clear enough. Her breathing had been labored and she'd heard her own arousal in her own voice. She'd been shaking, her nipples had been achingly hard. And then she'd rushed off to the bathroom to touch herself!

"Caroline," her own exasperation was just about all she could feel, while she pressed her hands against her thighs. They were shaking from the sheer willpower to hold everything in.

Caroline, though, seemed to miss her inner-struggle completely. "And what box is better left closed? What's better left unsaid?" She pushed, her voice growing louder, more distraught.

Caroline drew her hands through her hair, leaving the shoulder-length locks tousled and sexy, as she stared at Hannah with wide, wanting, dark eyes, her chest heaving.

And Hannah didn't think – barring the night at the lake house – that she'd ever wanted anyone more.

No, she *knew* she had never wanted anyone more than this. Had never wanted anyone like this.

She wanted Caroline from the deepest, most urgent part of herself in this moment, and as Caroline's words edged on begging…

Her gaze fell to Caroline's lips, and she couldn't stop herself.

Her hands reached out of their own volition and cupped Caroline's jaw. That strong, sharp jaw that she'd wanted to touch for years; it felt just like she'd always imagined it would against her fingertips.

Pulling Caroline against her, she lowered her mouth to hers, and everything inside of her went off like fireworks behind her closed eyes.

The kiss was light, just touching, as she committed it all to her senses. She didn't know for quite how long she'd wanted this, but she knew that with another brush of Caroline's mouth against hers, that nothing had ever felt so – real. So raw. So important.

Caroline groaned into her mouth, and she felt it everywhere, as she pushed Hannah back until she felt herself hit the wall, and the urgency of it sent a thrill through her whole body. Yes. Yes, she wanted to feel the potent desire she knew Caroline had inside of her, wanted to feel all of that passion directed at her.

The line had been crossed, and so many thoughts raced through her mind like flashing lights.

There were so many what-ifs, so many places this could go wrong, so many unknowns ahead.

But, as Caroline gripped her waist and rolled her hips into Hannah's own, igniting this arousal that burned right through her, she knew there was no going back. There was no taking back this level of want, no matter where it brought them.

It was scary.

It was –

It was so good, as she whimpered against Caroline's mouth.

December 25 – Last Year

So, it was scary.

It was scary to want someone so much, Hannah could acknowledge that. It was scary to love someone as much as she loved Caroline and know that Caroline had the total power to destroy her.

But after the last six weeks, she'd faced those fears and found that they were generally easy to handle when she handled them *with* Caroline.

Caroline, who moved at her pace with every step of their relationship. Caroline, who looked at her with latent desire, but still kissed her softly and stopped at Hannah's first sign of pulling back.

Caroline, who had made the most beautiful declaration to her days ago. Caroline who, unlike Hannah, had a way with words, and her words had landed so strongly in Hannah's chest, they felt like they cradled her heart.

Caroline wanted so much with Hannah – she wanted everything, in her own words.

And while Hannah wasn't sure she could leap into that same place with Caroline, she knew that there was no one else she would ever take this chance with. No one else she *could* ever take this chance with.

There was only Caroline who inspired this feeling in her.

And that's why she leaned in and kissed Caroline, right in front of Abbie, swallowing her own worries.

That, and because Caroline looked so cute with the mistletoe in her hand and trying so hard to cover the fact that she wanted to kiss Hannah.

And because Caroline had offered this morning not to come over, to give Abbie and Hannah their time – Caroline respected her. She respected Hannah and she respected her space with Abbie, and Hannah…

Hannah didn't necessarily love to think of the future; she was much more of a here and now kind of person, at this point in her life. If her marriage had taught her anything, it was that the future was entirely uncertain and pinning it on one person – especially too soon – was dangerous.

But even with the uncertainty of the future ahead, she wanted Caroline. And she was ready for Abbie to know that.

Plus, it had felt like forever since she'd kissed those lips. She knew it had only been about fifteen hours since they'd really kissed yesterday, but… fifteen hours felt like so damn long to go without.

She loved cupping Caroline's jaw. It was an absent thought she had as she stroked her fingers along the lines and brought her lips to Caroline's, reveling in the softness. Letting the comfort of her kiss overtake the slight nerves she had over Abbie's reaction.

"I did it!" Abbie's shout registered a second late in Hannah's brain. The words didn't matter so much as the happy tone, and that made Hannah smile as relief slid through her.

She pulled back from the kiss and took a second to revel in the heavy-lidded, dazed smile on Caroline's face. A visceral satisfaction worked its way through her, because *she* did that. She caused that look.

It was only then that Abbie's actual words registered to her, and she turned to look at her daughter in confusion, though she kept her hand on Caroline's, interlocking their fingers as she asked, "Honey? What do you mean by that?"

Abbie was literally dancing around the room, though, pumping her fists in the air, with a smile so big, Hannah was positive her cheeks had to be sore.

Caroline turned to face her, sitting so close on the couch that her entire body pressed against Hannah's side and she reveled in the feeling. The look of wonder on her face shifted into amused question as she gestured at Abbie dancing around.

Hannah could only shake her head; she had no clue. Only, "It seems like she's happy about us?"

Caroline's smile slid over her face slowly as she turned to look at Abbie who shouted, "Science works!" Before she turned back to look at Hannah.

"And you're… okay with this? With her knowing? With everything?" There was a hopeful edge in her voice that Hannah didn't miss.

She believed in here and now, Hannah thought again. And as she sat in the little apartment that *she* had found, that *she* paid for, with the woman she fell in love with, and her daughter laughing from sheer joy, and…

"I'm more than okay."

Life was good right now. She didn't know what the future would bring them, but it was good now.

January 5 – This Year

She didn't realize it, but the ball rolling them into the future really began on her birthday ten days later.

"Thank you," Hannah murmured as she cupped Caroline's jaw and tilted her head up toward her own.

This was her favorite thing to do. She'd admired Caroline's face so much, for so long… she loved having the right to stroke her fingers over it as much as she liked. It felt sacred for her, in a way she couldn't describe with words she didn't have.

"Thank you?" Caroline asked in a whisper, blinking with heavy lids in the way she had whenever Hannah got so close like this.

Hannah reveled in that. It was so incredibly heady to be able to see the effect she had on Caroline, on a woman who was so strong and capable of anything. But a big part of what made Hannah trust her feelings for Caroline was that… she could see Caroline had just as many feelings for her as Hannah did right back.

"Thank you for giving me the birthday I wanted." She drew Caroline up onto her tiptoes again and slid her lips along Caroline's full, pink ones that opened slightly against her own.

It was so easy to sigh into that kiss, into Caroline's kiss, and just let herself enjoy it. There was no ulterior motive here, there was nothing else here except for just this. Wanting. The two of them sharing a connection.

"It wasn't much," Caroline murmured against her mouth as they parted, just a bit.

Still feeling lost in that sensation, Hannah kept her eyes closed and processed the words for a few long moments. She fluttered her eyes open and shot Caroline an incredulous look. "You and Abbie made me breakfast, we had a lunchtime cake you two made, you arranged for Abbie to have a sleepover that she is *thrilled* about so we could have some time alone, you took me out for dinner, you bought me a present…" she trailed off, staring up at Caroline in bafflement.

Caroline shrugged and shuffled on her feet in that adorable way that she only ever did with Hannah. She'd never seen Caroline look unsure, except with her. In a way, it was incredibly and utterly flattering. She reached up and tucked a stray strand of hair behind Hannah's ear. "It was only a portfolio case."

Hannah shook her head quickly. "I love that portfolio case!"

And she did. She was entering into her final semester to finally complete her architecture degree, and this semester meant a full internship that she'd landed at one of the best firms in Boston. She knew she was only an intern, and she knew she was the oldest intern there.

But she loved it, and she was so damn ready to jump in. And most of all, she loved that she was with someone who supported that.

"I told you that I didn't want any presents, anyway. That I didn't want anything big or expensive," she reminded Caroline, holding her gaze to assure her that she had been honest.

"And I know you meant it," Caroline tossed back in a light, joking-but-not-really voice. "And why," she added in a murmur.

They didn't say it aloud, but she kind of loved that with Caroline, she didn't have to. She didn't have to voice that it was because… that being with Michael, her birthdays were extravagant. His assistant would remind him of her birthday – she was sure that was how he never forgot – and she received luxurious gifts.

Thousands of dollars spent on all kinds of jewelry, on the latest iPhone, on designer shoes and purses and perfume. Reservations for the most expensive fine dining.

Hannah had had all of that. Meaningless gifts and dinners of small talk and silent resentment. She's had all of the finest material items, buying her acquiescence to go along with every bad thing.

She knew Caroline's gifts would never be meaningless, she knew that any dinner wouldn't be spent in bad company. But... she just wanted to be herself. And Hannah, herself, didn't want or need anything like that. Anything extravagant.

She wanted... she just wanted this, she thought, as she looked down at their intertwined hands and looked out the large windows of Caroline's condo that allowed the moonlight to come in as it reflected off of the water in the wharf that her North End home gave a view of.

The night had been quietly perfect. It was everything she wanted.

Caroline cleared her throat and bit at her lip as she squeezed lightly at Hannah's hand. "I know that you meant that you didn't want anything crazy extravagant or anything. But... I did sort of get you one more thing."

She toyed with the neck of her sweater with her free hand, and Hannah's gaze fell to it. She licked her lips. Yes, this *wanting*... it was still new to her, despite feeling it for months. And the hunger she had, to take Caroline – and especially to be taken *by* Caroline – was certainly new for her.

"I thought you were joking about the lingerie," Hannah managed, her voice husky as she stared at Caroline, her mood easily shifting.

"What?" Caroline's eyebrows drew together in confusion before a look of dawning crossed her face and she quickly removed her hand from her collar. "Oh! No. I didn–" A dangerously sexy grin flashed over her face. "Well, there is some of that, too. But that's not what I was talking about now."

Excitement flared through her, compounded by the sheer excitement that not only did she feel desire so strongly, but she felt it for Caroline. Who really, really was an amazing lover. And that Caroline wanted her back, just as much.

If not more, it felt like. Impossibly.

"No?" Hannah asked, trailing her fingers up to Caroline's jaw again and then lightly down her neck, leaving goosebumps in her wake.

They'd only started having sex in the last three weeks, and she certainly never wasted any alone time they had together, sparse as it was, living with a ten-year-old. Hannah had most definitely had big, big plans for their evening.

Caroline's breath stuttered for a moment, squinting her eyes as if to find clarity. "I – no. I do have some big plans for us tonight." She leaned in, nipping at Hannah's earlobe before whispering hotly against her ear, "They involve making you come in my mouth, right here where you sit."

Hannah swallowed hard, heat pooling low in her stomach. "I think we could skip to that now."

Caroline hesitated and stared at her mouth, which Hannah knew meant she was truly contemplating it. Before she shook her head and squeezed her eyes closed. "No, no, this is – it's important." She reached over to the coffee table and picked up the portfolio case, handing it back to Hannah. "You didn't actually open it."

Hannah took it back slowly, curiously, shaking her head as she did so. "You shouldn't have gotten me anything else."

There was something about it, about Caroline buying things for her or providing too much for her that Hannah couldn't quite put into words – the curse of her life, it seemed – but it made her stomach twist unpleasantly.

Caroline pressed the case even closer toward her. "It's not… just open it. You'll see."

Hannah slowly undid the – undoubtedly expensive – leather straps that held the portfolio case together and flipped the top open. And then stared down at…

"An empty plot of land?" She asked, confused. But that was definitely what the picture she was staring at was.

Caroline cleared her throat and turned slightly to face Hannah on the couch as she explained, "It's a plot of land I bought three years ago, in Belmont. Really nice area, short commute into the city, and I had just paid off my condo and – I want a house. It's always been my plan to build my own home, and I just realized a few years ago that there was no point in waiting for a perfect time. There is no perfect time for things; I should do them when I want to do them. I'm turning thirty-six this year and by the time that happens, I want to be in my own home."

Her heart absolutely thundered in her chest and she blinked down at the papers in her lap. "I – and you want me to–"

"Design it." Caroline flashed her a self-deprecating grin. "You know I can't do that, myself. I have certain things I'd really like," she gestured to the paper she'd paperclipped to the top of the glossy plot of land photo, with a bullet-pointed list in Caroline's handwriting. "But I don't really know how to configure it all? Art is just not what I'm good at." She bit her lip and gave Hannah the sweetest look of confidence. "But you're amazing, and I trust you to design something beautiful. Everything I've ever seen you draw is magnificent."

Hannah's cheeks flushed warmly at that – especially because she certainly did not forget that the majority of what Caroline had seen of her drawings was Caroline herself.

"You… you really trust me to design your home?" She whispered and the words slot into place inside of her.

Caroline trusted her. She respected her knowledge and she trusted Hannah to be capable in ways that Hannah sometimes didn't even trust herself. No one else – especially not her last "partner" – ever made her feel that way.

"Of course I do," Caroline said, voice soft and soothing as a breeze.

Hannah blinked down at the land. It was nice – green grass, wooded area off to the side, a place for a long driveway…

She tilted her head, and she could see the home slowly building in front of her eyes. A nice wrap-around porch – Caroline would like that – big enough for a gazebo corner and a porch swing. A large office for all of the many times

Caroline chose to work at home rather than in-office, just on the first floor, through a den.

The home came to life in her mind easily, and her fingers already itched, but she merely rested them on the photo of the land as she smiled at Caroline. The warmth she felt inside of her radiated through her smile, she was positive.

"You want me to get you a pencil now?" Caroline asked, and her tone was only half-joking.

Hannah *did*, on one hand.

But, as she shook her hair back and stared at Caroline's perfect profile, she carefully reached out and put the open case on the table. "No," she murmured, "We'll get back to this later."

Within seconds, she had her hands in Caroline's hair and was straddling her waist as she kissed her deeply, sliding her tongue deep into her mouth.

She knew Caroline had plans – *I'm going to make you come in my mouth* – but… well, it was Hannah's birthday. She should get what she wanted, first.

February 13 – This Year

Hannah hadn't been excited about Valentine's Day for… quite some time, if she was being honest.

The last Valentine's Day she'd looked forward to had been before Abbie was born, with Michael. He'd taken her to New York City for a weekend of Broadway and five-star restaurants and a view from the penthouse of the most luxurious hotel she'd ever seen.

To her, at twenty, that had been the height of romance. It had been the romance novel, the beginning of a forever, of being swept off her feet, happily ever after.

At thirty-three, her views on romance were very, very different.

The thought drifted through her head as she leaned back against the counter in her small kitchen and watched Caroline and Abbie sit at the table together. Their heads were leaned in close, as Abbie demonstrated exactly how she wanted Caroline's help making a complex glittery Valentine's Day card.

God, Caroline was *so* not crafty. The thought made her snort quietly to herself, as well as the fierce frowny concentration lines that settled between Caroline's eyebrows.

At the sound, Caroline whipped her head around. "And why aren't you aren't helping with these, huh?!"

Hannah held her hands up in defense. "I was informed that this was an activity between the two of you. Far be it for me to interrupt."

Abbie shook her head. "Mom's making a ton of cookies for the bake sale, she's too busy to make the valentines for my classmates."

"And why are we making them the day before? Shouldn't we have started this, like, a few days ago?" Caroline poked Abbie jokingly in the side.

Abbie gave her a bright, overly-innocent smile that made Caroline break into her own.

After another few moments of watching Caroline try to glue a cut-up piece of doily, Hannah pushed herself off of the counter and walked up behind her chair.

Leaning down, she inhaled the scent of Caroline's shampoo, and her eyes fell shut for a moment.

It wasn't getting old at all. She'd thought maybe after a few months, it would. But it didn't.

Snapping herself out of the moment, she wrapped her arms around Caroline's and gently took the glue from her hands and slid the valentine away from her, as she murmured into her ear, "You can win any legal case, you can conquer the heart of every blonde female in this home, and you can fly around in that superhero cape you have, but I think we've found your weakness."

She easily glued down the doily piece in the design Abbie picked out for her Valentines as Caroline turned her head so that she was only centimeters from Hannah's face and she whispered, "Show-off."

Hannah turned to look at Caroline and even though Abbie was there – she knew, she'd known about them for the last eight weeks, but Hannah was still careful to keep things light for her daughter. Hand-holding and some cuddling on the couch. A few kisses here and there, but usually greeting or saying goodbye.

This was pure, unadulterated, soft affection, overwhelming her in the best way as she pressed her mouth to Caroline's.

Caroline had some glitter in her hair, glue on her fingers from helping with these valentines, and Hannah didn't ever forget that Caroline hated these kinds of commercial holidays.

But she did these things for Abbie.

At the thought of it, Hannah pressed even closer and slid her hand to Caroline's neck, stroking there briefly before she pulled back and stared into dark eyes as they fluttered open.

This? *This* was romance.

***

Later that night, when Abbie went to shower, Hannah slid Caroline one of the valentines she'd ended up helping out with.

And then proceeded to laugh as Caroline groaned and buried her face in her hands. "Please, no more!"

Hannah giggled as she insistently slid the valentine closer. "I don't need you to assemble this one, I just want you to read it."

Caroline visibly perked up as she opened the card, and Hannah felt the anxious little flutter in her stomach as she knew exactly what Caroline was reading.

Caroline –
I've finished your blueprints if you want to review them with me tonight.
And by tonight, I mean after Abbie goes to bed.
And by "after Abbie goes to bed", I mean – would you like to stay the night?
Love more than you realize,
Hannah

The small smile on Caroline's face was worth everything as she peeked over the card and asked, "Stay the night? With Abbie here and everything?"

Slowly, Hannah nodded.

It was another step, Caroline spending the night when Abbie was home. Their whole nights together were limited usually to weekends where Abbie was with her grandparents or at a sleepover, but… but Hannah wanted more than those odd nights.

And the anxiety quieted as Caroline's smile grew wider.

That happened a lot, too.

April 4 – This Year

"*I* don't like it," were the first words out of Michael's mouth when Hannah picked Abbie up from his house on Easter Sunday.

Hannah pursed her lips at him, ignoring the comment easily, as she'd taken to doing in the end of their marriage and in the last two years since she'd left him. "Where's Abbie? Is she ready to go?"

Michael sighed, his jaw clenching as he stepped closer to Hannah, doing that thing where he towered over her. He was five inches taller than she was, vastly more muscular, and she'd seen him lose control of his temper enough over the years, physically striking out at objects around him – and one time, slamming his fist right through the drywall next to her head. So close, she'd had plaster in her hair and she'd choked on the particles in the air in front of her face – that it had frightened her before. For years.

It still gave her the whisper of fear, of nerves, slithering through the bottom of her stomach. But instead of cowering back as she had done in the past, she took a deep breath and tilted her jaw up at him.

"I *said* I don't like it. I did the nice thing, Hannah, and I've let your relationship with Caroline go for the last few months–"

She didn't bother to hold back her snort. Michael's definition of *letting it go* was to make derisive comments and disgusting, snapping jokes whenever they'd talked on the phone. Which, admittedly was not much since the holidays. He'd had his weekend with Abbie right before Christmas, when he and Caroline had had an altercation, and then he'd been in Europe for almost two months.

When he'd returned six weeks ago, he'd only seen Abbie only because his parents had picked her up for the weekend and he'd gone to their home to take her out for the afternoon. And, that was it.

While Hannah on a personal level was more than glad – ecstatic, relieved, unburdened – by her lack of face time with Michael for months, it was the precarious situation of having a child with the man. Because Abbie always *felt* every canceled plan and lack of action to spend time with her.

Her disbelieving snort incensed him even more, as the vein in his forehead started to pound. "I don't know what the fuck you think you're doing, but Caroline Parker is spending too much time with my daughter. I thought, if I let this run its course, you'll get this shit out of your system and–"

"Mom!" Abbie called from the top of the stairs, and Hannah deliberately pushed against Michael's shoulder to create space between them and push a smile onto her face at her daughter.

"Hi, honey. Why don't you get your bag and we'll go home? I have your favorite mac and cheese ready to have with the ham tonight."

Abbie nodded and scrambled off to her room. Hannah found that it was disturbingly easy to slip on the smile and fake-light voice for Abbie, in ways she hadn't had to do since they'd left this home. It used to be so simple, so second-nature to do it… maybe that was why it felt so disturbing now.

Because now she really knew how not *normal* that was.

She took a deep breath and turned back around, and she could see that the fact that she had physically pushed passed Michael had not only made him angrier, but shocked him, too. It shocked her a little as well.

She would have never done that during their marriage.

With the way his fists clenched and shook, she could see he was close to his boiling point. This?

This would have undoubtedly been the time she backed down in any fight when they'd been together, no matter what it was about.

"Hannah, I swear to god, you'd better listen to what I'm fucking telling you." He reached out and clamped his hand around her wrist, the hold tight and edging past uncomfortable into painful.

And that? Incensed her, now, in a way that it would have terrified her, before.

Drawing herself up to stand as tall as she could, she stared him in the eye. "You have no right to tell me what to do. Never again. I spent ten years listening to you, but that portion of our lives is over now." With a grimace, she wrenched her arm out of his grip. "And if you ever put your hands on me again, you will regret it." The strength filled her now, filled her enough to say the words that bubbled right up: "Trust me; I have a *really* good lawyer."

The fact that she'd shocked him beyond action and words as Abbie came running down the stairs, zipping up her jacket as she went, gave Hannah a satisfaction she didn't think she'd ever felt before.

She wasn't sure, but she thought his blood might actually be boiling, as she opened the door for Abbie as her daughter said goodbye to Michael over her shoulder. Hannah didn't share the sentiment, and shut the large oak door that had always felt so much like a cage door locking her in a prison, behind her.

No matter what the future held? *This* was the past.

May 21 – This Year

"*Oh* my god," the words left Hannah on a whimper.

"*Shh*," Caroline shushed against her neck, before she slid her tongue all the way up to Hannah's ear. She nipped at her earlobe and slid her hand to grasp at Hannah's thigh, just under the hem of her graduation robe. "We have to be quiet."

She slid her hand up, taking the hem of Hannah's dress with her.

"We shouldn't be doing this here," she panted out as she threw her head back against the door, pressing herself closer to Caroline in spite of her words.

Her cap had been on the ground as of two minutes ago, when they'd crashed through the door of the classroom.

It had all started because Caroline, Abbie, and Robyn had met up with her in the near-empty building where most of her classes were located, to get pictures of her in her cap and gown while she was on campus.

She'd felt embarrassed at their enthused insistence but had posed nonetheless.

Then, when she'd said she had to go inside to get her purse where she'd left it after one last congratulatory meeting with her professor, Caroline had offered to accompany her, while Robyn and Abbie headed the next block over to Fenway Park to nab their seats for the commencement ceremony.

As soon as they'd entered the empty classroom, Caroline had been on her.

Hands grasping at her hips, mouth hot on Hannah's, as she'd pushed her up against the wall and was just *so* hungry for her.

"Do you want to stop?" Caroline asked, her fingers pausing just before they slid to Hannah's inner-thigh.

And even though she knew they *should* for a multitude of reasons – anyone could walk by, she had to be at the commencement ceremony in less than a half hour, Abbie and Robyn were there waiting for Caroline already, they were in a *classroom* – Hannah blinked open her eyes and looked at Caroline.

Those eyes that were dark with absolute want, but the question was earnest. Hannah could say no, now or at any other point, and Caroline would stop.

But... she bit her lip as the arousal beat steadily through her veins.

Hannah shook her head as she spread her thighs, and she could feel herself clench in anticipation of being touched.

Caroline was a dreamy lover. She paid attention to every reaction Hannah had; she touched her like she'd tuned Hannah's body just for her fingers.

"Touch me," she whispered, her voice shaking with excited need.

Caroline immediately slid her dexterous fingers to Hannah's inner-thigh and then up... up...

Hannah's head thumped back against the wall but she didn't feel a thing and she gasped out a breath, as Caroline touched her.

She rubbed her clit through Hannah's soaked underwear, and Hannah didn't know how Caroline had this power over her. How she could suck and nip at Hannah's neck so intuitively. Like she knew every button to hit to make Hannah so ready.

"There's something about you like this. You look so sexy," Caroline husked into her ear, as she reached back and grabbed Hannah's ass, pulling her impossibly closer. "God, I'm so proud of you. You're fucking perfect."

Caroline's words and the heady sentiment behind them ratcheted Hannah up even higher, the feeling in her stomach winding tighter and tighter.

But it wasn't enough. It wasn't enough. The thought echoed through Hannah's mind as Caroline rubbed her harder, faster. She dug her fingers into Caroline's back, her hips grinding down into her hand.

She could come like this, she knew she could. Her thigh was already shaking as the heat streaked through her body, while Caroline's mouth went back to her neck.

She could come like this, but – it wasn't what she *wanted*.

"I want..." She trailed off, a groan working out of her throat.

"What do you want?" Caroline snapped her head up, slowing her fingers but not stopping. She waited for Hannah to open her eyes again before she repeated, "What do you want?"

It was the knowing arch of her eyebrow that really did it for her. There was a power Caroline had, not just as a lover, but as a *person*. She knew Hannah and in a lot of ways – a lot of scary ways that Hannah didn't always allow herself to think about – but when they had sex, it was always so good because of it.

Caroline knew what she wanted. She knew what Hannah craved since the moment she'd heard Caroline describe holding down her lover at the lake house. She'd tried to put it into words the first time they'd had sex, but hadn't necessarily been great at it.

But over the last few months, she'd gotten a bit better at communicating that want.

"I want you to take me," she breathed, moving her hands up to tangle her fingers into Caroline's soft waves. "Really fuck me."

The words still made her flush a bit, but the way Caroline's breath left her quickly in a strangled moan made them so worth it.

She didn't need it all of the time, but there was something about the day. About the *bigness* of it, about what it meant, and the weight of it was huge. In a good way, but it was a lot and she wanted...

She wanted to feel Caroline in it, everywhere. All over her. She wanted to feel close to her, so close to her, tied to her, and Hannah didn't know how to put into words what exactly she needed, but luckily Caroline seemed to get it.

She slid her hand back down Hannah's thigh, and though she ached for her touch, she felt the anticipation shiver through her.

"That's what you want?" Caroline asked, grasping Hannah's hips with a firm hold and tugging her up from where she was leaning against the wall.

She easily maneuvered to stand behind Hannah, her hands going back to her hips, for which Hannah was grateful. Her legs already felt weak and she knew they were going to get even weaker.

Caroline walked them forward to the front row of desks, pressing herself against Hannah's back.

She was the perfect height now, to rest her chin just over Hannah's shoulder and whisper, "Bend over. And grab the edge of the desk."

Hannah's whimper was choked as the electricity shot through her body and landed right between her legs. She did as she was told, that anticipation rushing through her even more, until she quivered with it.

Caroline slid one hand up her back, over her dress and gown, until it rested between her shoulder blades. Not really applying pressure, but letting Hannah know that it *could*, and just that feeling had her spreading her legs even wider.

She closed her eyes and it made everything feel even… more. Especially as Caroline slid her hand up the back of her thigh, under her dress and –

She groaned as Caroline swiftly pulled her underwear to the side and slid two fingers into her.

Fuck.

She filled her slowly, giving Hannah a moment – she always did – and as soon as Hannah unconsciously pressed her hips back into her, Caroline pressed down slightly with the hand on her back to stop her.

She felt Caroline lean over her back, driving her fingers even deeper, and Hannah cried out.

"You need to be quiet, though," Caroline whispered against her neck, her hot breath falling against Hannah's skin, making her shudder.

"I'm–" She couldn't speak, her mouth opening with no words coming out, only the sounds that formed in the back of her throat.

She was about to fall apart, she was going to come, she loved Caroline, she trusted her.

"I know," Caroline assured, groaning herself as Hannah felt herself clench.

God, it felt so good. So good. So good.

Hannah moaned again; she couldn't help it. She couldn't help it with these sensations wracking through her body. Especially not when Caroline worked her other hand down Hannah's front and moved up her thigh to touch her clit.

"You have to be quiet," Caroline commanded against her ear. "Anyone could come in and see what I'm doing to you."

Logically, she knew it wasn't true. She knew that the door had a lock and that Caroline had shut the lights and locked it. But it still made her whimper weakly as Caroline fucked her harder.

"And I don't want anyone to see you. I want to be the only one who does this to you, who gets to see you like this," Caroline continued, her voice so low, and Hannah could only nod.

She bit her lip so hard to keep in her sounds, her hands gripping the edges of the desk until her knuckles turned white, and when Caroline rubbed her clit faster, keeping those fingers buried inside of her she, she –

"*God*!" She couldn't stop herself as she fell over the edge.

Everything seemed to flip upside down, the world blurring at the edges while she rode out the pleasure, working her hips against Caroline's hand jerkily.

It didn't stop, the sensations running through her body for what felt like long, long minutes, while Caroline nuzzled at her neck, giving her soft kisses.

At long last, Hannah's body totally relaxed and she laid against the desk with a contented sigh.

She loved the feeling of Caroline completely against her, her heart beating against her back.

"You are, you know," she whispered, surprising herself. She often planned for the words to come out of her mouth and had to really sit with them first. But not these.

"Hmm?" Caroline hummed, before she straightened and slowly removed herself from Hannah, using her palms to smooth out her dress and gown.

Hannah nearly choked when Caroline slid her wet fingers into her mouth. She didn't do it often, but Hannah still wasn't used to it. Or how hot it made her. Hannah had to sit back on the edge of the desk to gather her strength for a minute.

She cleared her throat when Caroline grinned deviously at her and gestured for her to continue.

"Um – I was just… I mean. You are – you're the only one who gets me, like that. Has ever gotten me… like *that*."

Uninhabited. Wanting. Needing. Uncaring about what she looked like or what she sounded like.

She'd only ever slept with three people before Caroline. Her high school prom date whom she'd gone on a few dates with, a boy at a college party her first year, and then Michael. And she'd never really gotten out of her own head with them enough to be in the *moment*, and had definitely never felt comfortable enough to voice these wants.

And truly, she'd never wanted to feel overpowered in any way by them. That was something she'd maybe fantasized about by herself, but never saw herself doing with someone else.

Until Caroline.

Feeling a little exposed, she pushed herself off the desk and took a deep breath as she brushed her hands over herself, trying to figure out if there were any wrinkles she had to smooth out.

There must be, even though she'd ironed it –

Caroline reached out and stilled her hands. "You're the only one who gets me like this, too."

Hannah arched a disbelieving eyebrow, because…

Caroline rolled her eyes at herself. "Maybe not necessarily when it comes to sex itself, but – *me*."

There was such sincerity in her voice, it melted Hannah's dubiousness. Melted it right into a soft smile.

That lasted until her eyes caught on the clock on the wall behind Caroline's head. Shock and alarm raced through her, making her jump. "I have to get into the lineup in ten minutes!"

She made it just in time, nine minutes and forty-three seconds later. Hannah excused her way through the mass of caps and gowns, until she got to her place next to Karla and exhaled a deep sigh of relief.

"Hey, I expected you to be here like a half hour early, with snacks," Karla joked before she took a good look at her.

Hannah watched as her eyebrows lowered, abject confusion flashed over her features, and then a shocked, knowing look took over.

Oh, boy.

"Don't you look... well taken care of." She sniggered behind her hand.

And honestly? Even as she blushed, Hannah really didn't even care.

It was a good day. Her body was still thrumming from coming so hard, her heart was brimming, and she was about to finally graduate with a degree she earned.

As her row was called, her stomach twisted in nervous excitement, and she took a second to close her eyes and take a deep breath, as she thought of her mom. She would have been so, so excited. This was a moment she'd wanted for Hannah, for a long time, as someone who had never quite graduated from high school herself.

Hannah took in a deep breath and could remember just how proud her mom had looked at her high school graduation, right out in the crowd. So *proud*.

Seeing her cheering there... well, Hannah still remembered it, fifteen years later.

Opening her eyes, she peered up into the stands, exactly where Caroline had texted she was. It was close enough that they would have a really good view, Caroline had said. Which meant it was close enough that Hannah could see them, too. And she needed it.

She caught sight of Robyn, then next to her where Abbie sat, and her heart swelled a bit. Even more when she locked eyes with Caroline.

What really surprised her, though, was when she realized who was sitting next to Caroline.

Caroline's parents, and her brother, Jared, too. Even after he'd asked her out and she'd politely turned him down – not even realizing at the time that she'd had a crush on his sister, but she *had* – he'd turned out to be a very good friend.

She had to blink away unexpected tears as her name was called, and she watched her little section clap and cheer. Somehow in the last year and a half, she'd gone from having only Abbie to a section.

That maybe meant just as much to her as the diploma. Maybe more, even.

This was exactly what Hannah had been striving for, this door to be unlocked. It had been a dream of hers, locked up for years, and now – she'd done it.

She'd really done it.

July 4 – This Year

The future she was scared of didn't really hit her in the face until summer.

"Mom, the *pool*!" Abbie shouted.

Hannah laughed as she watched her daughter excitedly belly-flop right into Caroline's pool.

Not the pool at her condo, like where they'd spent last Fourth of July. But the one that had been completed as of last week at Caroline's house.

The house that was almost completely done. Hannah had been here to see the construction stages with Caroline a few times, and the speed with which it was put up over the last couple of months was truly astounding.

But, as Caroline reminded her with a cute little grin, she was pretty good with codes and laws.

Also, she'd helped a foreman at one of the best construction crews in the city with his divorce, so that certainly didn't hurt.

Hannah had finished her design for Caroline's home before even Valentine's Day had hit. She'd been so taken with designing it – she knew Caroline so well, knew what she wanted in a home, what she needed.

The entire design had completely slipped out and she'd shown it to Caroline – completed – within two weeks. Caroline had been utterly thrilled with it, and it had been genuine, too.

Hannah could tell.

The construction had started by April.

And now, even though the house wasn't *quite* live-in ready but was so close, Caroline had excitedly offered to host the Fourth of July cookout at her new home.

She was happy for Caroline, she truly was.

Especially because she could see how proud Caroline was of the house, as she took her family and friends on tours of the home. She was practically vibrating with excitement as she'd come up behind Hannah to ask, "Can I take you on your personal tour, now?"

Hannah shook her head in amused exasperation. "The tour I took with Abbie and your mom earlier wasn't personal enough…?"

Caroline playfully narrowed her eyes as she took Hannah's hand in hers and tugged her up to stand. "Not nearly personal enough as I want to be with you."

She stood with Caroline easily, though, because if Hannah was going to say she wasn't excited to have a moment alone with Caroline amidst the crowd of the day, she'd be lying.

Caroline took her in through the kitchen and then up the stairs – the house still needed a few finishing touches. Paint colors that she knew would look bold and eye-catching, much like Caroline herself, the doors to the three bedrooms upstairs, the faucet in the guest bathroom. All small things that didn't take away from the brilliance of the house itself.

"The only thing everyone else hasn't seen – it's too small for a grand tour, and I really wanted to only be here with you anyway," Caroline murmured as she laced their fingers together and led Hannah through the master bedroom.

It was spacious with large windows that overlooked the yard and the woods. Plus, the French doors led to a small balcony, because she knew Caroline would enjoy that. And apparently, it was the balcony Caroline wanted to show her, throwing her a beautiful grin as she gestured for Hannah to go out the door first.

It was stunning, Hannah thought as she walked out onto the balcony as the sun was setting on the horizon.

"My dad's going to light the fireworks soon," Caroline whispered conspiratorially, wiggling her eyebrows in the cutest and most ridiculous way.

Her mouth fell open in exaggerated offense. "That's illegal in the state of Massachusetts!"

They held eye contact as they broke down in laughter, and Hannah walked forward to the railing and slid her fingertips over the intricately carved wood.

"It really is beautiful," she whispered, moving her hands over the railing again and closing her eyes, taking in a contented deep breath as Caroline came up behind her.

"It is. Thanks for designing it." Caroline placed a light kiss against her hair.

Hannah shook her head, though. "You knew what you wanted."

"But *you* brought it to life. It wouldn't be nearly what it is if I hadn't had you there to read my mind."

Hannah felt a smile tug at her lips, and she just let it. Caroline often wanted her to accept a compliment, and she was working on it.

She could feel the deep breath Caroline took against her back, and she turned in her arms to look down at her curiously.

The look on Caroline's face was soft and affectionate but also laden with nerves. Hannah could recognize that expression, and the implications with what it could mean immediately popped the bubble she'd spent the day in. The last two months in, really, ever since graduation and getting a job at an architecture firm.

"So," Caroline began, taking in another deep breath and nodding to herself. "I'll be moving into the house within the next couple of weeks. And... I'll be missing you and Abbie, and having such quick access to you guys, and you to me."

"It's less than a half hour away," Hannah was quick to say, especially as that feeling edged in even sharper.

She'd felt it – just a bit – when Caroline had given her the picture of the plot of land. But it hadn't come up again in the last six months, and it weighed on her now like a stone.

Especially as she watched Caroline reach into her back pocket as she shrugged. "I know. It's not really far, but it's different."

Hannah had to swallow hard, feeling her palms start to sweat and her heart begin to race as dread lodged in her stomach. What was coming out of that pocket?

"And I was thinking..." Caroline drew out a key.

A key.

It was a key?!

"Caroline, we can't move in with you," the words rushed out of Hannah, because this had been something that she'd been fearing.

That with Caroline's house coming together and their relationship going so well, because it *really* was, that this would be next!

Caroline froze, key in hand, as the soft smile on her face fell. The feeling of causing that look mixed with the dread already in her stomach, she... she swallowed hard but pushed on.

"I mean, you and I are– we're so good together."

"Yeah," Caroline echoed quietly.

"We are, but I... but things are so good right now, the way they are. Everything in my life is falling into place the way I'd always dreamed of." It was. She had her daughter, and she had her degree, and the job she actually enjoyed, and she was financially starting to see a light at the end of a very dark tunnel. "I can't, that *can't* change."

It couldn't. She couldn't jeopardize that, and her blood was rushing in her ears, and–

"I wasn't asking you to move in," Caroline said, her voice low and perhaps the most dejected Hannah had ever heard it.

Hannah's hands, midway through dragging through her hair, fell to her sides. And she ran through the conversation and realized Caroline was right. She hadn't asked.

Embarrassed – she could hardly ever get the words out, but this time when they flew right out of her rooted in fear, it wasn't even what she'd thought – Hannah could only stare for a long moment. "I'm... I'm sorry. I saw the key, and I thought..."

"You thought that I was asking you and Abbie to move in with me," Caroline filled in the blanks, but her voice was still full of that hurt tone. "And your immediate thought was a very defensive speech to tell me no."

Hannah squeezed her eyes closed while her heart felt like it was being squeezed in her chest.

Still, she nodded. And of course, now was when she felt at a loss for words. "I didn't– I'm sorry."

"I don't want you to be sorry for the way you feel," Caroline said, and Hannah could tell she meant the sentiment, even with the empty sound in her words.

"I'm just, I'm not ready."

Caroline nodded slowly as she reached out and put the key on the railing. "I only wanted to give you the key, so that you knew you could come here whenever. If you needed anything or when we have plans or…" She cleared her throat and blinked quickly. "You don't have to take it."

Hannah opened her mouth once, then twice, but nothing came out. She didn't know how to phrase the feeling that clogged up her throat and made her heart flutter with anxiety at the thought of next steps and futures.

She didn't want to apologize for her words, but for hurting Caroline's feelings. Those words didn't come out, either.

She could see the way Caroline's jaw worked, clenching, as she swallowed hard and stepped back. Hannah could feel the extra inches between them, painfully.

"Here's the thing, Hannah. I'm not going to ask you to move in or to marry me–"

Marriage?! The word stole Hannah's breath all over again.

"I'm not going to do any of those things until I'd be one hundred percent sure that you're ready, because I'm never going to push you into them. I know that's not now and honestly, I'm not sure when it would be. So, I'm not asking," Caroline repeated, mustering up a small smile that dug right into Hannah's heart with how it was just a bit *off*. "But… it did still hurt a little to hear."

"I'm—"

"Don't apologize," Caroline murmured, quirking her lips into a half-smile, one that spoke of gently hurt feelings and quiet understanding that Hannah was never quite sure she was worthy of.

"It hurt to hear. But, technically, we've been together for less than a year. You've been officially divorced for just over. I want you, Hannah, in every way. I think you know that."

Hannah did. She could feel it, feel loved in a way that she'd never imagined before.

She didn't know how to put in words all of the feelings she had around that, around how it made her feel. Around how that kind of even added to her nerves while it also made her feel beautiful, adored, warm, anxious, undeserving… a whole myriad of emotions.

All she really knew for sure was that she didn't want this to change anything. Not just in her life, but between them. Because what they'd found here between them, exactly as they were, was perfect.

And she was really, really nervous about messing with perfection. Because to Hannah? Good things – perfect things – felt tenuous. And she was so very wary of what could come next.

August 8 – This Year

"*I* don't know about you, but I miss the cupcake birthday party," Caroline said through a huff of breath as she put her hands on her waist and tilted her head up at the lanterns she'd hung up around her yard.

"Hey, at least it's for a book," Hannah cajoled and blew out a breath as she put her hands on her own hips and looked around. "A book-themed party – could be a lot worse."

A slow smile pulled at Caroline's mouth. "Yeah, you aren't wrong." She turned and gave Abbie a warm smile, and Hannah didn't even think she realized she was doing it. As always, that warmed Hannah.

"Plus, the book *was* pretty good."

Hannah lifted her eyebrows in surprise. "You read it?"

The it in question was *Divinity* by Blair St. James, about a thirteen-year-old girl who uncovers a world of immortals. Abbie had been obsessed since Norah loaned her a copy on the Fourth of July.

Hannah knew that the book wasn't hugely popular, so she did wonder if Abbie's friends would even know what they were walking into tomorrow. But she mostly hoped it didn't have a negative effect on the big day.

"It's all Abbie's talked about for the last three weeks; color me intrigued. I read Blair St. James' Ivy Abrams books when Melissa was really into them a few years ago, and she's a pretty good writer. If she had an adult series, I'd read it in a heartbeat." She shrugged, before she let out a light laugh. "I don't know what it says about me that I barely have time to read in my free time, but when I do, I read books intended for pre-teens and children."

"I think it mostly says that you care about relating to the kids in your life that you care about," Hannah said softly, admiring the curve of Caroline's cheekbone in the way the sunset reflected off her light summer tan.

"Caroline! Mom! Look – I got the fence to look like the gateway into the Evermore!" Abbie called from across the yard.

They'd been decorating Caroline's yard for all of the materials that would be fine overnight, before Abbie held her party tomorrow in Caroline's backyard. Which they were making into the Evermore, aka the place the Divine beings lived in the book.

It was, admittedly, a decent amount of work. But Abbie was thrilled and had been doing a lot of the groundwork for the design and the ideas for materials herself. Hannah was pretty proud of that, actually.

"Might I also remind you that you had the idea for the book theme and to have it in your own yard?" She nudged Caroline's shoulder with her own as they walked over to see Abbie's latest in décor, and then stayed close enough to just touch Caroline, feeling her body heat.

It didn't matter that the night was already warm and a little humid. She liked the closeness. Caroline, she thought, did too.

"This looks so cool, Abbacado," Caroline commented, and Hannah could hear the genuine tone.

"It really does, honey." It really did. Her daughter, the genius.

"Thanks!" Abbie bounced on her feet a bit in her excitement.

"I'm thinking we should call it a night, though. Getting late, and we have a ginormous day tomorrow," Caroline wiggled her eyebrows as she spoke the thoughts on Hannah's mind.

As they carried the remainder of the decorations inside to finish in the morning, Abbie hummed before asking, "Would you want to be a Divine? Like, live forever?"

"Depends," Caroline answered thoughtfully, tapping on her chin. "Do I have you two?"

Abbie nodded in affirmation, and Caroline checked her with her hip as they entered the kitchen through the back slider. "Then, I'm down. Where do I sign up?"

She was using that tone, the light and joking one she often used with Abbie. But there was a truth in those words that slithered through Hannah's stomach with unease.

The word *forever* did that to her.

"You didn't answer, Mom," Abbie turned her gaze to Hannah.

Who placed her hand on the top of her daughter's head and tilted it back to look into bright blue eyes. "I'm already going to love you forever and ever, honey." She smiled when Abbie gave her the look that said *you're killing me*. "Why don't you go get ready for bed?"

They were spending the night at Caroline's so they could get up early and get ready for the party. And Abbie never made it any secret how much she loved when they had a sleepover at Caroline's.

Tonight was no different; Abbie let out a whoop of excitement as she turned from the room and scampered upstairs, singing about her party.

"That was an interesting answer."

She'd already pulled out one of the cleaning cloths from under the sink to start wiping down the counter when Caroline spoke. She turned to look at her, seeing Caroline's amused lifted eyebrow.

Hannah just snorted softly and sprayed the cleaner along the marble countertop as she shook her head, feeling the hair from her ponytail brush against her neck. "Well, I don't want to ruin my daughter's enjoyment of her current favorite book by talking about how being with anyone forever just isn't real."

Caroline was silent for a few long moments – much longer than would be typical for her – before she said, "Well, I think on the bright side, Abbie knows the concept of *Divinity* is just fiction."

Her voice was quiet, though, lacking its usual verve. Hannah looked across the kitchen at her to see her face, but Caroline wasn't facing her.

The seed of unease? That, however, settled.

August 23 – This Year

"*How* many people here remember my Grandpa Frank? My mom's dad, for anyone who doesn't know. About this tall," Caroline held her hand up to just above her own head, a charming, humorous smile on her lips as she stood in front of the crowd at her parents forty-fifth wedding anniversary party.

"He passed away about fifteen years ago. But he was a crotchety old man most of the time, and even though he was a very fun and loving grandfather, he *always* loved to talk about how he had been so sure that there was no way my parents' marriage would last. Not because he didn't like my dad, but because he was absolutely adamant that they were too different and that eventually, it would fizzle out. I mean, he said this to us – their children!"

The crowd laughed as Caroline made a face, exacerbating the oddness of the story, and Hannah did too. Caroline was a natural public speaker – she had a way of weaving together a narrative and drawing people in to listen to her. She was utterly enthralling.

"Well. I did love my Grandpa Frank, and I thought he was typically a very smart man. But in this instance, I think even he would be happy to eat his own words. Because when I look at you two, so happy together after so long? I can see that you have what everyone wants." Caroline shared a look with her parents before she chuckled, "Thank god, too, because I'm not sure who I would represent in the divorce."

Hannah chuckled along with everyone else and raised her glass of champagne towards Tricia and George.

Caroline had done the legwork in planning their anniversary – because, of course she had – and it had all come together beautifully, at a reception hall Caroline had scouted out for the event months ago.

And the work she'd put in had really paid off.

Caroline strode toward her, wearing a dress for once. It occurred to Hannah that she'd never really seen Caroline in a dress, always in suits. And her throat went dry in both, she'd realized earlier.

She smiled up at her in affection. "That was amazing."

Caroline ducked down and pressed her lips against Hannah's cheek. "I try. Especially because none of the Goon Squad was going to make a good speech and we all knew it."

Hannah snorted at Caroline's nickname that she'd revealed she'd called her brothers when she was younger. She'd told Hannah while they'd been laying in bed a few months ago, early in the morning, as Hannah had toyed with Caroline's fingers and asked her about what growing up had been like with three siblings.

It was a curious topic for her, as someone who'd grown up an only child, married an only child, and was currently raising one.

Caroline slid into the seat she'd been occupying next to Hannah, giving her a small smile as the music queued up and started playing *Can't Help Falling in Love*. Caroline turned her attention to her parents as they danced, her grin turning unbelievably soft and sweet.

Hannah, however, watched Caroline closely.

There was *something* else that came over her features as she watched her parents dance.

Something that Hannah couldn't quite put her finger on, but it made her anxious, deep inside.

There had been moments like this, quiet moments, for the last couple of weeks. Maybe longer, if she was pressed to think about it.

But Caroline never said anything, so she'd pushed it out of her mind. Hannah's modus operandi in her last relationship had been to not rock the boat as much as she could, generally.

That conscious thought, that she was comparing her current relationship with Caroline to her past with Michael, slammed into her like a freight train, and she jerked upright, heart pounding in her chest with the realization.

Caroline turned to look at her in alarm. "Are you okay? What is it?"

Hannah took in a deep breath to try and calm the pounding of her heart, before she shook her head. "Ah – I…" How did she bring this up? How did she talk about this? She closed her eyes and gathered as much strength as she could. "Uh. Everything's fine."

Before Caroline could push – in that way she had, that soft, inquiring way – Hannah shook her head. "Do you want to dance?"

Even if they were going to discuss… whatever they had to discuss, here and now was not the time and place. And quite honestly, she would be lying if she said that a big part of her was very worried about whatever conversation they would have when they finally addressed whatever was a bit *off* with Caroline.

She'd much rather try to forget about that for a while and just be close to her.

Caroline was still giving her a slightly doubtful look with that slight arch of an eyebrow. Before she nodded and held out her hand for Hannah to take.

She did.

They really hadn't done this before, it occurred to her as Caroline's hands fell to the small of her back. Their bodies aligned easily, and Caroline was leading her, in one fell swoop. Hannah rested her hands at the back of Caroline's neck, toying with the soft hairs that had escaped her updo.

They hadn't danced like this before, she thought again, sighing in contentment as they moved easily. She'd never been led in a dance by someone that was shorter than her, she registered, with a little smile.

It fell a bit when she angled her head down and saw Caroline looking at her parents with that weird look on her face again.

Hannah's stomach sank.

***

Hours later, when they'd returned to her apartment and Abbie had completely zonked out from the night out, Hannah took a second to lean against the doorway as she stared at her daughter.

She used to do this when she needed to find her core and take some strength. It didn't really help at the moment, as she turned and went back to the kitchen, where Caroline was making them both a cup of tea.

Squeezing her eyes closed, Hannah just pushed the words out, "What's going on?"

Caroline hummed, as she finished typing something on her phone, before looking up at Hannah with a little grin. "Nothing, I was just making a note that you're almost out of sugar. I'm going grocery shopping tomorrow, so I'll just grab you some."

It would be so easy to drop it now. So easy! She wanted to. She really wanted to. When her life was going well, she didn't want to change it. And she knew change could lead to good things – their relationship being a great example – but it unnerved her.

But, as per her therapist's words, her default setting was often to cope in situations even when she knew they weren't quite *right*. And it was something she'd been focused on not doing ever since leaving Michael.

Taking in a deep breath and rolling her lips to gather herself for a moment, she shook her head.

"No, not about sugar. Or tea. I mean… what's going on with you? There's – there's…" Cursing herself, she cleared her throat. "There's just been a look on your face sometimes. In the last few weeks, but before that, too. Maybe not as much, before that? But, it's there. There's something there."

It was the best she could do, and she blinked at Caroline as she bit at her lip, because Caroline understood her. She knew she did, even if she wasn't eloquent.

The way Caroline's movements as she finished steeping the tea slowed but didn't entirely stop, the way her head tilted down in acceptance and acknowledgement at the words... she *knew* it.

It ate at her, the anxiety filling her.

Caroline braced her hands against the counter and drew in a deep, deep breath through her nose.

"Okay. I didn't realize I was that easy to read." Her attempt at the joke wasn't good, and they both knew it.

"I don't know how to break it to you, but when it comes to everything not including work, you're about a middle school reading level for me." And she was approaching elementary school level as the months went by.

They stood in silence for long moments as Caroline turned around and leaned against the counter, tilting her head back as she faced the ceiling. The obvious tension in her shoulders, even from feet away, made Hannah's own body tense.

"I'm not saying this to push you or rush you into anything. But I guess in the last few weeks, I've been really thinking about... where we're going."

"What do you mean?" Hannah asked, her throat running dry immediately.

Caroline pushed herself off of the counter, starting an agitated pace across the limited floorspace.

"I mean, whenever I bring up the future or us getting more serious, it's like I'm hitting a boundary with you. You like us the way we are–"

"I do," she was quick to interject, her heart starting to hammer in her chest. "I *do*. I love you, I love us. I don't want to lose you."

It was the absolute truth. Such a truth, Hannah felt it with every breath she took.

"But, do you want a future with me?" Caroline's words were firm, but quiet. They were unyielding, and knocked Hannah's breath from her lungs. It aligned right with the look in her eyes, that intense, passionate look. "Because I want that. I want the future. You know? *The* future." A beautiful, heartbreaking, fleeting smile flitted over her face. "The one where I can talk about you and Abbie moving in with me sometime in the relatively near future, the one where I can say with confidence that no, we aren't getting engaged soon, necessarily, but *sometime* in the future, yes. So I can say that when my family asks me – because they do ask – and know that it's actually the truth. The future where I can say that I want to be with you forever and not have that look cross your face. That look, right there," Caroline quickly pointed at her.

Hannah hadn't even realized she had been making any face, but she knew Caroline wasn't making it up.

Especially not when she felt everything, so messy and big inside.

"I – it's…" She pressed her hands against her stomach, hoping the action would help settle it. It didn't. "It's not that I don't want *you* or us, or this," she was able to say, quickly, and that was the utter truth. A burning, serious, desperate truth.

But her other truth was undeniable. "I just don't believe in *that*," she whispered.

Caroline faced her, looking for all the world like she was braced for something. "Don't believe in what, exactly?"

"That…" Hannah licked her lips, her hands fluttering uselessly in front of her. "That happy ever after, together forever, kind of thing."

"You don't?" Caroline asked, her voice low and vulnerable.

Hannah swallowed hard, hating the sound of doubt in Caroline's voice. Her stomach tangled with anxiety of this conversation, over the way she felt, over what it might mean for them, and over the idea of this hurting Caroline when it was the very last thing she wanted. God, it was enough to make her want to be sick.

"I don't. I just – I got married to Michael and I was young and naïve and I…" she trailed off, waving her hands in front of her as if they could explain what she was feeling. God, she hated getting like this!

She heaved a deep breath, aggravated at herself, as she raked her hands through her hair. *Calm, be calm and think.* It helped her find the words a few moments later, keeping her voice low, if a bit strained with the distress she felt. "I believed in people being together forever, then. When I got married to Michael. I did. I was swept away with the romance of it all." She could see it clearly in her mind, and she shook her head at her past self, disgusted and embarrassed. "But I learned very quickly that it was all – it's all… it's just something to believe in. Some sort of fairytale."

The look on Caroline's face was so crestfallen and disappointed, it cracked something in Hannah's chest that she didn't know she even had anymore. The silence between them made Hannah's heart race, her stomach bottom out, and she didn't think she'd ever felt this nervous with Caroline. Never.

"Then what are we doing here?" Caroline asked softly, dark eyes looking up into Hannah's, searching.

And Hannah's heart tripped and a sickening dread took a chokehold at the implication of her words. "I… we – we're together. We love each other and we…" With the pounding of her blood in her ears and her anxiety notching up even higher, her throat grew too tight to push out words.

She totally floundered, especially as Caroline nodded, seemingly to herself.

"Right," Caroline's voice was so quiet, it barely reached Hannah's ears. "Okay." She didn't make eye contact with Hannah, though. Instead, her eyes were trained over Hannah's shoulder, her eyebrows drawn down low and crinkled, as she continued to nod. "Right."

"What does that mean?" She asked, voice just louder than a breath, but it was all she could manage.

"It means," Caroline rubbed her palms over her eyes, hard, before releasing and taking a deep breath. "It means, that I want the forever. I want to get married. I want these things, and I want them with you. So, I think I just need a minute to reconcile some things."

Hannah's breath left her completely, her throat feeling like it was grabbed in a vice grip. What did it mean?

No words left her, though, before Caroline quietly said goodbye and shut the apartment door behind her.

**

What in the world did *a minute* mean?

Hannah wondered it all night.

**

Her eyes snapped open before seven in the morning the next day, after only three hours of a fitful sleep.

The thing was, she was so unfamiliar with the feeling in her stomach. In her chest. Like she was going to be sick, aching like she was missing something. Something precious and warm.

Something like Caroline.

Groaning, she rubbed at her eyes and slipped into her robe. "Abbie, honey?" She spoke softly as she lightly knocked on the door. It was early for a Sunday, but Abbie was often awake just as early as she was. "I have work in an hour." It was the occasional weekend that she would still pick up a shift at The Bean Dream. "And I'm going to drop you off at–"

She caught herself before she said Caroline's name. Should she still do that? Bring Abbie over to her on their routine Saturdays? They weren't broken up, right? How would she explain that to Abbie?

God, the double-hit of the thought made Hannah close her eyes so tight and force in a deep breath.

Shaking herself out of it, she opened the door slowly. "Honey?" She asked a little louder. "I'll make you something for breakfast. Sunday morning waffles?"

And still, silence in the dark room.

Not even the mention of waffles had Abbie up? That was entirely new.

Hannah flicked on the light, squinting for a moment as she adjusted and –

And then the bottom dropped right out from her world, as she saw the empty bed. "Abbie?" She asked again, panic making her voice raise.

It was foolish to search the bed – it was empty – but she did just that. And then look under. Then in the closet. The bathroom, living room, kitchen… all empty.

By the time she darted into her bedroom for her phone, she could barely unlock it with how hard her hands were shaking.

And then relief shot right through her body so strongly, she thought she could have melted right then and there.

3 missed calls – Caroline <3

Caroline <3 – 6:43AM

Hey, I don't know if you're still sleeping or if you just don't have your phone on you, but Abbie's here.

She's okay.

She barely remembered how she got to Caroline's, hardly remembered the drive there at all. Did she shut the car off in the driveway?

Still in her pajamas, she swung the front door open and almost fell to her knees at the sight of Abbie sitting on the stairs in the front hall of the house, leaning into Caroline. Almost like she was burrowing into her side, as Caroline had a comforting arm around her shoulder and cradled a cup of coffee in the other hand.

Her daughter was also still in her pajamas, and Hannah raced forward, tracing her hands over Abbie's hair, her face, and – and she looked like she was in one piece. "What…" She had to pause and take in a deep breath before she could manage, "What were you thinking? Leaving when I was asleep? Abigail Elizabeth Dalton, that is *not* okay."

She still had her hands braced on Abbie's shoulders as Abbie nodded, her bottom lip poking out in a pout. "Caroline told me that already. And she said I owe you a big apology, and I'm sorry I scared you."

There was a lot under the tone, but it was sincere.

She shot Caroline a grateful look above Abbie's head, really looking at her for the first time this morning and seeing how exhausted she looked, as well. "I woke up to a little person at the side of my bed who definitely did not fall asleep here so… that was new." The corner of her mouth lifted in a tiny smile.

The smile, small as it was, almost made Hannah cry. After their conversation the previous night and this morning with Abbie, a smile from Caroline was like the best salve.

Clearing her throat, she turned back to Abbie, worry and concern and frustration and relief and everything rolling together inside of her. "How did you get here? What were you thinking?" She asked again, her voice shaking with it all.

"I took the T and then the train and then walked. It's only a few blocks." Abbie looked up at her with a defiance in her eleven-year-old eyes that Hannah was completely taken aback by as she spoke with ferocity, "You can't break up with Caroline! You can't push her away from us! You *can't*!"

Hannah blinked, her hands feeling slack on her daughter's shoulders. "What?"

Breaking up? Her heart just couldn't handle that this morning, wrenching in her chest, as she jerked her head to look at Caroline, eyes wide. She didn't miss something last night, right? She hadn't.

Caroline didn't look nearly as poleaxed as she felt, and Hannah got the feeling she'd already heard this before she'd arrived. "Methinks someone was eavesdropping from her bedroom last night."

Hannah blew out a long-suffering sigh, even as the panic inside of her barely subsided. "Of course." She aimed a look at Abbie, because, "How many times do we have to talk about this? Not everything is meant for you to hear. Especially conversations like last night."

"But it matters to me, too! I had to come and see Caroline this morning to make sure everything was okay, because you wouldn't. I *know* you wouldn't!" Abbie tossed back at her.

And the reality of her daughter's words felt like a slap in the face. Not just because Abbie saw and knew and understood so much of her and her relationship, but because her words weren't born of a tantrum or having an attitude, and the utter anguish in them tore at Hannah's insides. She felt the tears prick behind her eyes, and –

She'd tried so *hard* to do her best by Abbie, her entire life. She'd tried so hard to shield her from everything Michael did. She'd tried so hard to make up for all of Michael's shortcomings. She'd been so hoping that her relationship with Michael and everything that entailed hadn't touched Abbie. She'd worked so hard, and… and Abbie clearly saw and knew a lot more than Hannah ever hoped.

God. She swallowed thickly, her breathing rough.

Caroline closed her eyes tightly and tilted her head back as Hannah's hands fell to her sides listlessly, unsure of what exactly to do in that moment.

"Abbacado, you shouldn't say things like that to your mom. You only get one, and yours is pretty great, right?" Caroline said softly and broke the quiet that had fallen around them in the last minute. Caroline's dark eyes were on Hannah's face, measuring as she patted Abbie's hip. "Why don't you take a breather for a few in the den? With the door *closed*."

She looked to Hannah for the final call, and she let out a deep breath and nodded.

Abbie frowned as she stood and informed Hannah as she wiped at her eye with a tired fist, "Caroline says – she said that if you two break up, that me and her aren't."

Like another punch right to the stomach and it left her breathless, just barely holding back the compounding of tears.

She waited until she heard the sliding door of the den close, before she asked, "Breaking up?" Hannah's throat felt scratchy and even though it wasn't even eight in the morning, she felt like she'd already had the longest day. "Is that... are we...? Because I–"

She broke off, wrapping her arms around her waist as she leaned against the wall. How did she put it all together in words, everything in her head?

"We aren't. I don't think." Caroline murmured, placing her coffee mug on the stair next to her as she rubbed her temple. "But, I'm struggling with the idea that I want these things and I want them with *you*, and they're all things that you don't want... with me."

Hannah closed her eyes as she raked her hand through her hair, anxiety making her movements jerky.

"And I keep wondering what I can do differently?" She narrowed her eyes in desperate thought. "I try not to push you because I *understand* how life was with Michael. And I know you were reluctant to start us because of Abbie, so I wonder if maybe that has something to do with it?" Caroline continued, seeming like she was almost talking to herself.

And Hannah could only shake her head.

Because at this point, it wasn't. It wasn't about Abbie.

Abbie had been her biggest reason to not give into these feelings in the beginning, and that fear was real. But now, almost a year into it, confirmed for Hannah a few things. Especially Abbie's parting words –

That Caroline was the kind of person who wouldn't stop talking to Abbie if things went wrong for them.

"It's about me," she said, her voice low. "It's all – it's me. There's nothing you can do differently."

There wasn't. Because Caroline was, as far as Hannah was concerned, as perfect as a person could be.

She started to pace slightly, feeling like everything inside of her was going a little haywire, and needed an outlet, as she started to ramble.

"Caroline, I only learned how to live independently a few years ago. I only reached a place of total independence, where I don't fall back and rely on someone else for any problems and for things to be handled for me in some way a year ago, after the divorce."

"I'm not trying to steal your independence," Caroline said, her voice exasperated and near to begging. "I told you, last Christmas, that I–"

"It's not about you and the way you love me, Caroline," the words erupted from her throat, finally. In a way she'd never been able to really get out from her head. "It's not about that *beautiful*, somehow dependable and exciting at the same time, totally encompassing and special… love." She didn't know when her tears had fully formed in her eyes, but she felt them drip down her cheeks at just how overwhelmed she could be by the intensity and strength of Caroline's love for her.

Because, it was overwhelming. It was beautiful and good and special, and… so much. So scary, even, to be loved in that way.

"Then what is it?" Caroline tentatively reached out to touch her shoulders and look her in the eye, and there were tears in her eyes, too. Those perfect dark eyes.

"It's *me*," she confessed, her throat feeling so raw. "It's me, Caroline. And the way *I* love *you*."

She should pull away from Caroline, she knew it, but she just didn't have the strength to. She didn't have to strength to move away from Caroline's, and wasn't that just the issue? The irony of it made her laugh, humorlessly, as she continued, "I fell into my life with Michael, and I know that so much of what happened wasn't my fault. Technically. I know that."

Especially with the therapy she'd had since the end of the marriage, that had helped her logically come to an understanding that it wasn't her *fault*. She still struggled, though, which was something she was still working through with her therapist.

The therapy she'd gotten thanks to Caroline.

The thought made her jerk back and away from the woman she wanted to lean on more than anything. She felt cold, she dimly registered, with the distance. With any distance.

"But, I allowed it to happen," the root of so many of her fears worked itself out in the world, in a terrified whisper. "I got to that point of dependence on Michael because it was so easy to just know that so many things could be taken care of. And that was with *Michael*!" Hannah drew her hands through her hair, choking on her breath as the desperation to make Caroline understand her took a tight hold.

She stared into dark eyes that watched her. They weren't accusing or angry or anything bad in any way, they were the polar opposite of the way Michael looked at her, and, "With you? *You?* You could handle every issue that ever came my way, you could pave the entire road for us before I even see how deep the bumps go. You'd do it easily and selflessly and because you love me. And I love it." She nodded with the passion in her words, feeling it lace through her veins, even as she had to wipe at her eyes again. "You would do anything for me, and it's who you are."

"But I am *terrified* that I will want it. That I will let it happen. No relationship I've been in – or even imagined – is the way it is, with you. Healthy and full and real and I…" she trailed off, feeling helpless. "I trust you, completely. I do. You would never want me to be less independent, you would never want me to be less than everything I can." Hannah knew that. She knew that was true, with every fiber of her being.

Caroline nodded at the sentiment, both vehemently assuring and looking so confused.

"I know you love me so much. I know you do; I feel it all of the time. And I'm sure you maybe think and feel that you love me more than I love you, but it's just not true." Her eyes rolled up to the ceiling, trying to blink back these tears now that just kept falling, irrepressibly. God, she didn't remember the last time she'd felt like this, so emotionally uncontrolled. "The way *I* love *you*? Is terrifyingly huge, Caroline. Way bigger than I know how to show you. It's just… it's *me* I don't trust." She repeated, this time the words feeling like a real confession. "Not yet."

"Not yet," Caroline echoed, staring at Hannah with something akin to wonder. "Not yet?" She gently – so heartrendingly tender – reached up and stroked her palm against Hannah's cheek. And, after feeling like she'd shown every card she owned, like she'd truly bared her soul, the touch felt so soothing.

Still, she felt like her heart was pounding out of her chest as she shook her head.

"I'm not ready yet to commit to anything more right now than that I love you and I want to be with you. But I can tell you that I'm terrified of losing you, and that *that* scares me more than the idea of an uncertain forever." Hannah leaned her cheek into Caroline's palm and closed her eyes at the accepting warmth. "Just don't give up on me. Please," she finished, *finally* feeling like she was able to take a deep breath.

Hannah didn't even realize it happened before her arms snaked out and wrapped around Caroline, pulling her so close in a hard, desperate hug. She needed to be close, so badly.

She'd never been so scared to lose someone before. It was a terrifying thought, especially when she considered her hard-fought independence. But... as she shut her eyes and breathed in the smell of Caroline's shampoo, as strong arms wrapped around her as well, she couldn't do without this now.

She *wouldn't*. It might take time, but she would work on it. "I can work on it."

"I think I'm going to need you to. I'm here, Hannah, and I don't want to go anywhere. Because, seriously, I love you more than I've ever loved anyone. But, I'm going to want more, in the future."

Hannah bit her lip and held on a little tighter. "I know."

There was still that knot in her stomach, but it loosened.

September 6 – This Year

Hannah jumped where she stood in the kitchen preparing dinner, as the door to the apartment opened and then slammed closed. Putting down the knife she'd been about to use to chop vegetables, she turned to walk down the front hall. "Hello?"

Only to pause with relief as Abbie stormed down the hall, coming to stand in the doorway of the kitchen. Her eyebrows were crinkled in a very rare, angry expression and before Hannah could even ask, she announced, "I don't want to go to Grandma and Grandpa's next weekend."

Wiping her hands on the dish towel she had hanging on the counter, she reached out to smooth her hands over Abbie's hair to study her face in confusion. "Honey, what are you talking about? What happened?"

Abbie typically always had a great time with Francis and Marina. Sometimes it was… stuffy, Hannah supposed was the best word for it. But she wasn't shocked, considering the silver spoons they'd both been raised with.

"They took me back-to-school shopping today and then you all talked about me spending next weekend with them and I don't want to." Abbie's hands went to her hips, bunching her T-shirt there. "I miss Gram."

At the mention of her own mother, Hannah felt the painful little zing right to her heart. "I do, too, honey. But–" She didn't have the chance to finish speaking her bafflement aloud before the apartment door opened again.

The distinct clacking of Marina's ridiculously expensive high heels sounded toward the kitchen.

"Abigail, do not run away or slam doors when your grandfather and I are speaking to you. Is that the manners with which you're being raised?" She arched an eyebrow at Hannah.

She grit her teeth at the familiar look. She got along better with Francis than Marina and always had, but dealing with both of them could be… trying. She knew that Michael's parents were civil with her for Abbie's sake and that she managed it back for the same reason.

Before she could say anything, Abbie whipped around to face her grandmother. "You – you said Caroline was not nice words, and I heard it!"

"*What?*" Hannah asked, the hot feeling of defense and irritation starting to work through her already, her hands landing on Abbie's shoulders for support as her daughter leaned back against her.

"I wanted to call Caroline and ask her a question and Grandma said no, and then – and then she asked where we went shopping for school stuff last weekend and I said that Caroline took us to stores near her house, and *she* said–"

"Do not point at me, Abigail, show some respect." Marina cut her off.

"*You* show respect!" Abbie said back, tilting her jaw up in defiance.

Marina's shocked intake of breath seemed to echo through the kitchen.

Hannah lightly massaged Abbie's shoulders for a few seconds and took in a deep breath through her nose to calm the angry, roiling feeling in her stomach. "Abbie, why don't you take a breather in your room for a few, okay? It's all okay, honey."

Abbie turned around and stared up at her, big blue eyes angry and right under that, a little vulnerable. "She said that Caroline was a predat – preda-tor y – lesbian and that she takes advantage of weak-willed people, and that–"

Feeling both gutted and slapped in the face with the words, Hannah managed to give Abbie the slightest, tight smile. "Just, go to your room, honey. I'll be right there." She waited until Abbie rounded the corner, before she turned back to Marina, hands falling to her own hips and let the anger sear through her. "You said *what* to my daughter?"

Francis' soft footfalls sounded moments before he appeared behind Marina's back, shaking his head already. His voice was low and placating, speaking over his wife. "Now, Hannah, she didn't say that *to* Abbie."

"I don't care! How dare you?" Hannah didn't know the last time she'd felt so... so livid. It pounded through her veins, on both her behalf and, even more, Caroline's. She could expect something like this from Michael, but – "We have always managed to keep a civil, if nothing else, relationship between the three of us. No matter what. I always assumed having a relationship with Abbie meant that much to you."

"Hannah, you know it does." Francis raised his hands in a gesture that read *calm down*.

Calm was the furthest thing from what Hannah felt.

"But am I supposed to sit idly by while my granddaughter is practically being raised by a woman who is taking advantage of a bad situation? A woman who screwed over my son? This woman is all Abigail speaks of half the time! She sees her more than my son gets to see her–"

"And the person you need to speak to about that is *your son*!" Hannah shot back, pressing her shaking hands tightly against her thighs, looking for control.

It didn't matter that they always kept these matters quiet between the three of them, that Michael was simply... never mentioned. It didn't matter that things between her and Caroline were still slightly off, from everything that had happened a few weeks ago. Not a lot, but just ever slightly.

Like Caroline was a little skittish, for the first time in their relationship, about what Hannah actually wanted.

And Hannah... she was skittish because she had to really figure out what she really wanted. And how to be okay with it.

But that didn't matter right now. They could have broken up, and it wouldn't matter in this moment.

"Abbie talks about Caroline so much because *Caroline* is here for her. When Abbie was up sick in the middle of the night with a scorching fever, and I considered taking her to the hospital a few months ago, your son?" The word fell from her lips with disgust. "Didn't answer the phone or even respond to my messages for two days. Caroline? Was here in a heartbeat. Because she is good and dependable, and she loves Abbie, she loves me, and she treats both of us better than Michael ever did. And you better get used to her, because if you want to continue spending time with Abbie? You need to accept that Caroline is going to be here, too. Probably more and more as time goes on. Why don't you see how weak-willed I am, then?" She challenged, the words falling from her lips before her mind could even catch up to them, pushed on by sheer feeling.

Hannah wasn't sure who was more shocked out of the three of them, as a tense quiet set over the kitchen.

But she straightened her spine and held firm, because she believed in what she said. In every word. And she would be damned if Michael's parents would ever determine who she was or what she was going to do.

"And? Don't speak to Abbie about Caroline, *ever*. I think you've seen now how that will work out." She inclined her head toward the hallway Abbie had walked down.

Where she would bet her meager life savings that Abbie was only just around the corner right now, anyway.

Francis put his hand on Marina's tight shoulder, as they both knew she would be the one likely to argue with Hannah.

"We'll call," he informed her tersely.

"Don't call before you think about everything I said," she shot back as they turned around.

As they walked out, she took in a deep breath and blew it out, feeling her shoulders still stiff with the interaction. And, honestly, the anger. How dare they say anything like that in front of Abbie? About *Caroline*?

She wasn't shocked at their opinion, because she knew the Daltons. But she'd thought that after keeping everything so very civil through the divorce that they would continue to do the same afterwards.

"Well, that was... something else," Caroline's voice drifted to her, and for a second, Hannah thought she was imagining it, in this high-emotion moment.

She snapped her eyes open and looked to the doorway the Daltons had just vacated.

No. She hadn't imagined it.

Caroline stood, with a questioning smile on her lips, wearing dark jeans with a cute, short-sleeved shirt tucked in and she looked – perfect.

Hannah felt a bit of embarrassment rise as she rolled her lips, and the words she'd just had so easily fell away. "I just..."

"Forgot you invited me over for dinner?" Caroline guessed, keeping her voice light, but it was very clear she'd heard the entire interaction.

The smile Caroline sent her from where she stood, the real, full, loving smile – the one that wasn't missing or strained in any way – had the power to make the haywire feeling inside of Hannah settle. It was the first not strained in any way smile she'd received in a few weeks, and it loosened that final knot.

That was a smile that really said, *everything will be okay. We will be okay. The future will be okay.*

And for the first time in a very, very long time, Hannah believed it.

October 31 – This Year

"*That* was the *best* trick or treat," Abbie commented, her voice a little shrill from the excitement and the fact that she'd been eating bits and pieces of candy for the last two hours and was still practically vibrating on her feet as they walked up the footpath to Caroline's front door.

It was the second Halloween in a row that very few people had recognized Abbie's costume – the main character from the *Divinity* book – but she hadn't cared. Especially because Norah was also a character from the book, and they'd excitedly planned their costumes in conjunction with one another.

"Seriously," Caroline agreed with Abbie, "The best trick-or-treat."

"That's just because you stole all of our Milky Ways," Norah said over her shoulder with a laugh at her aunt.

"And I had a great time doing it!"

Hannah just shook her head at all of them affectionately as she opened the door. "Okay, girls, it's only seven. What do you want to do now?"

"Norah's going to come play in my room and we're going to go through all of our candy!" Abbie grabbed Norah's hand and the two of them started running up the stairs.

Having her arm looped through Caroline's, Hannah could feel how she tensed as the girls' footsteps disappeared up the stairs under the din of giggles.

Hannah spun on her heel to face Caroline, arching an eyebrow at her, concerned. "You okay? What's this whole tense feeling about?"

She really needed to know, because they hadn't really had any of those sort of tense moments in over a month.

Caroline's eyes searched hers. "Uh, just – what Abbie said made me a little…" She trailed off, arching a questioning eyebrow at Hannah.

Who replayed her daughter's words over in her head until she realized what Caroline was talking about. *My room*.

"Her room," she murmured, tasting the words on her lips, the permanence of it making her feel a little tense herself.

It would be easy to stop there, but in the last couple of months, she had so many talks about this.

The future was going to come no matter what, and she wasn't going to push anything, but she wasn't going to stop it, either. She couldn't.

But she had to… embrace the forward steps as much as she could.

She and Abbie stayed the night at Caroline's usually at least once a week. Sometimes more. And Abbie had a room that Caroline furnished with Abbie's input, where Abbie kept several belongings.

It… it *was* her room. Pretending otherwise would be a disservice to herself, Caroline, and Abbie, all at once.

"Her room," Caroline repeated, watching Hannah closely, eyes a little guarded.

Even though she got the slightest worry niggling in her stomach, she swallowed hard and nodded. The smile that worked itself onto her lips wasn't forced, even if it was a little riddled with nerves.

"Unless you know another kid who's sleeping up in that room on the nights that we're not here…" she trailed off and offered a laugh that showed her nerves, but – it wasn't like she could hide them from Caroline anyway.

She met Caroline's searching gaze head-on, not backing down at all from the intensity there. And she didn't try to mask anything she was feeling, either.

All she knew was that in reward for her honesty and maybe her bravery – because perhaps it wasn't really brave, but it felt like it, to Hannah – Caroline smiled brightly. She slid her hand into Hannah's hair, the hold warm and strong and familiar, as she tugged Hannah down.

She went with it easily, wanting, as Caroline rocked up onto her tiptoes and pressed her lips against Hannah's, the kiss warm and enthusiastic, tasting just a bit like chocolate.

And something in her kiss quieted those nerves. Hannah found herself genuinely smiling as Caroline pulled back.

"On this day last year, you called me baby. So maybe last Halloween was better," Caroline whispered, her dark eyes glinting with happiness.

Hannah shook her head. "Do not call the day you were injured like that the best day. It's not allowed."

"I love when you lay down the law," Caroline teased, before she pushed up onto her tiptoes again and nipped at Hannah's jaw. "Why don't I show you to my room while the girls are occupied?"

Hannah's hands landed on Caroline's hips as she blindly followed her lead.

November 24 – This Year

"*What* was I even thinking? *Sure, Ma, I'll host Thanksgiving?*" Caroline lamented with a comical imitation of herself. "I don't even *like* Thanksgiving! And now all of those people are going to be at my house all day!"

Hannah looked over at her, taking note of the dejected look on Caroline's face as she stared at her hands helplessly. Covered in flour, as she'd been attempting to rollout a pie crust. *Attempting* being a very key word.

She had to hold in her laugh, as she dried her hands on the hand towel she'd had thrown over her shoulder, and swiftly moved over to Caroline's side. She looked at the… somewhat recognizable as a crust dough and coughed to cover up her chuckle.

"First, you were thinking that your mom was very stressed about dealing with the volume of people coming tomorrow, second you were thinking about how much you love showing off this house, third, *those people* are your family," she couldn't help the bit of incredulous laughter that escaped her throat at that. "And third?" Hannah lifted her eyebrows and waited for Caroline to look at her, before she finished, "Sweetheart, you are always volunteering to host things. I think it's lovely," she informed Caroline honestly, ducking down to kiss the cheek that wasn't streaked with flour.

Though, she licked her lips, there was a bit of cinnamon there, somehow, even though it had been Hannah who had made the snickerdoodles an hour ago.

"Very sweet," she whispered, before she kissed the warm cheek again, and took a moment to breathe Caroline in and feel how easily Caroline's back settled against her front.

With a light, content sigh, she patted Caroline's hip and stepped back to her side of the counter.

"Now, I appreciate all of your attempts at helping for the last hour, I really do." And, she did. If she was pressed to think back to her marriage, she knew she would find exactly *no* times like this ever where Michael ever cooked with her. Not out of either the desire to assist her to lighten her burden or to simply spend time with her.

And she knew both of those were factors for Caroline.

It made everything inside of her warm as she reached out and started curling Caroline's "dough" into a ball to determine just how far gone it was. "You said you have some work to do tonight to make sure you can have at least a couple of full days off. So, why don't you go finish that up right now and I'll get everything ready, so that tomorrow, it will be smooth sailing?"

Caroline huffed out a breath, her hands falling adorably, indignantly to her hips as she turned to face Hannah. "I can't just volunteer to host Thanksgiving and then saddle you with all of the work!"

"Well, it so happens that one of us has today, tomorrow, and Friday off from work, nothing hanging over my head, and…" Hannah bit her lip and exaggeratedly looked between herself and her girlfriend, "That one of us also happens to be far better at the culinary arts."

"I can cook!" Caroline defended, her mouth falling open in what Hannah could tell was mock offense.

She laughed as she nodded. "Right, of course."

"I can! What do you think I did before you came along?"

"Take out and struggle?" She suggested, biting her bottom lip against the full-blown smile that wanted to take over.

Caroline narrowed her eyes. "Oh, I see that's how it is. I'll have you know, Ms. Raised-in-her-mom's-diner, I can get along just fine for myself!"

"Spaghetti, tacos, and grilled cheese notwithstanding."

"You are deliberately discrediting all of my specialties," Caroline grumbled as she scrubbed her hands in the sink.

"And what would you have done for a Thanksgiving meal if you didn't have me?" Hannah arched a smart eyebrow at Caroline.

"Take out and struggle," Caroline parroted, before she looped her fingers into the waist of Hannah's jeans and leaned up on her tiptoes to press her lips against Hannah's. Softly, just enough for a taste, before she pulled back. "Thank you. I'll be in the office; shouldn't be that long. I'll figure out what to do for dinner tonight since you're doing this."

Hannah just shook her head after Caroline, watching her ass as she left the room.

All right. The dough.

As she started adding a bit more flour and kneading it out, she let her mind drift a bit into their conversation. Even though she'd mostly been kidding, because Caroline *was* extremely capable, Hannah did do most of the cooking.

She and Abbie had dinner here at least three times a week, usually four or five. And the thing was, she loved it. She loved cooking in here, for and with Caroline and Abbie. Doing something she was good at, that relaxed her, and having every single one of her efforts appreciated. Even if it was just a simple preparation, Caroline always sung her praises.

She knew Caroline was already singing her praises about Thanksgiving, and the food wasn't even cooked.

But tomorrow would go so well. The flow of the house was set up perfectly for having family and friends over – Hannah had deliberately designed it that way, knowing Caroline. She could very dimly hear Abbie in the living room from where she was, and had the perfect view out into the back yard.

It gave her a certain pride, really, knowing that she'd designed this. Because, really, it was the perfect house.

She hummed to herself, feeling more than content, as she didn't even have to look to know she was in the right place as she used her right foot to tug open the drawer with the trash, before spinning and taking two steps to utilize the island counter.

This counter, with one side designed perfectly for cooking and the other with a slightly lower edge, designed for people to sit and keep the chef company, was something Hannah had always dreamed about.

The kitchen in the small apartment she'd grown up in had been filled with delicious food, warm laughs, and plenty of family meals between herself and her mother. But it had been cramped, outdated, and with very little counter space. The kitchen she'd had at Michael's house – it was beautiful, but it never felt quite like a home. It was never warm and welcoming.

This kitchen, it was everything Hannah would have ever wanted. Right down to the breakfast nook in the corner, the built-in fridge that blended with the cabinets, the quartz countertops…

Everything came to a halt as she realized that *she'd* designed this kitchen. Logically, she knew she had, of course.

But… she had designed it… for herself.

She'd jumped into designing this house for Caroline and it went so well, because she had the clearest vision.

But – but Caroline really didn't care so much about the kitchen, did she? No.

Hannah had designed it all, for herself. Because *she* was going to use it. Because she saw herself here. For a whole plethora of future moments yet to come.

The thought had her staring blankly across the kitchen, amused, baffled, nervous, and… she wasn't quite certain how to put the feeling in words. The way her stomach clenched and her nerves jangled.

And she wondered just how much she'd subconsciously put of herself into other aspects in this house.

Into subtly planning a future here.

December 11 – This Year

Hannah was confused when she stepped into the house and didn't immediately hear a movie or a tv show playing, or talking, or laughter, or even music.

Caroline's car was in the driveway and the door had been unlocked, so…

"Hello?" She called out as she unwrapped the scarf from her neck and didn't even need to look as she tossed it up over the hook of the coatrack.

"Hi," Abbie's voice drifted in from the den, sounding… off.

She walked down the hallway in confusion, peering into the den to see Abbie sitting alone, with her arms crossed and her backpack sitting at her feet.

A very, very weird sight to behold, indeed.

On an average day, Hannah's arrival often could be construed as through she was interrupting something. She didn't ever *feel* like that, because there were fewer things that gave her as much pleasant warmth – as much sheer happiness – as Caroline and Abbie's relationship. Even if Caroline was working and Abbie was reading or playing a video game or watching tv, they felt connected.

Hannah's deliberately light concerned smile of greeting at her daughter dipped completely as she walked closer. Her eyes flicked over Abbie, taking her in to note that there was nothing physically wrong… before her alarm really started to sound. "Honey, what's going on?"

Abbie let out a sigh and splayed her fingers over the couch cushion as she shrugged. "Nothing. I just finished my homework before you came in. I'm ready to go."

Now there was definite alarm and confusion – Abbie had never once been *ready to go* from Caroline's. "Huh?" She *must* have been mistaken. "You're ready to… go? Did you have dinner?"

She couldn't imagine that was the case, it wasn't even six yet. Normally they all had dinner together once Hannah got home.

"No. And we didn't put up the decorations. Or open my cookie advent calendar, either," Abbie relayed in her whiny voice, with a pout. A deep, deep pout, with the lines on her forehead that she got when Hannah could tell she was feeling particularly petulant.

She was blessed to have a daughter that she proudly considered top-of-the-line. A daughter who was sweet and kind and resilient and funny and intelligent. But, Hannah was all-too-aware that Abbie was also still very much a child.

A child who had stayed up particularly late over the past weekend at two-night sleepover, as well. And an Abbie who get very little sleep? Was a grumpy Abbie.

"What happened?"

"I didn't do anything!" Abbie was quick to insist.

Hannah only hummed and stroked a quick hand through her daughter's hair. "Well, you can stop looking like you're ready to run out the door, because I'm going to talk to Caroline before we do anything else."

She found Caroline in her office, with the door almost nearly closed. Not quite, just a few inches open, but even that was odd for Caroline, unless she was on a call.

So, so incredibly odd, she thought again with a frown, as she opened the door to peek in.

Only to find that Caroline wasn't on a call. She wasn't even sitting at her desk.

She was pacing.

With a frantic sort of energy that Caroline rarely ever had. If *ever*? Hannah frowned as she thought – no, Caroline had never displayed this kind of frenetic nervous energy.

Which only deepened her concern and utter bafflement, as she cleared her throat to make her presence known.

Caroline whipped her head up so quickly, Hannah was genuinely worried she would strain her neck. And instead of the normal loving, soft smile that warmed her face, there remained a clear anxiety over those sharp features that Hannah so loved.

"*What* is going on?" She asked, keeping her voice down because she would bet a lot of money that Abbie was out there having as much of a listen as she could.

Caroline – who had just *never* looked this strained – fluttered her hands around in a hopeless gesture. "I – I don't know! It wasn't like any of our normal days."

Before Hannah could urge her to continue, Caroline did. They were different, the two of them; Caroline could always find the words.

"When we got back here after school, I told her that I had some work to do for a while. But that she could do her homework first and after we were both done, we could get out the rest of the decorations that she's been dying to put up," Caroline started, drawing up her shoulders as she recounted the story as seriously and studiously as if she were recounting the background to a legal brief.

Hannah found it endearing. She nodded – Abbie had a whole plan and layout of the decorations she wanted to put up all around the house, and they'd gone out a bought a ton of them, much to Caroline's chagrin. Though, she didn't seem to mind all that much this year.

Hannah found that more than a little exciting, herself.

"But she was so – mad? Normally, it's fine when we make little adjustments. And she has that book report that she has to finish by the end of the week on *A Wrinkle in Time*. She told me that we *had* to do the decorations first. Stomped her foot at me and everything!" The baffled, hurt look on Caroline's face made Hannah want to laugh.

She stifled it.

"But, I have a deadline, myself, I know that she has her own deadline, and the decoration fun isn't on a deadline. So, I just told her we aren't doing the fun stuff until we get the work done, and that's that. And she stormed into the living room and turned on the TV! So, I shut it off and said she can watch that when work is done, too. Abbie will spend hours getting lost in TV-world, and then nothing will get done!" Caroline's voice notched up.

Hannah nodded sagely to validate her. She *was* correct, after all.

"Then, she wanted to open the holiday cookie advent calendar after our after-school snack, and I said she can't have the desserts that we reward ourselves with when we haven't done our work, first. Now, she's mad at me and she informed me that I can't order her to do anything because it's not *my job*," Caroline finished, seeming to deflate, as sadness overtook her tone.

Hannah nodded again, slowly now, as she took a step closer to Caroline.

Who gave her the look of a wounded puppy. "Are you mad at me?"

That gave Hannah pause, as she shook her head and stared at her girlfriend in confusion. "Me? Mad at *you*?"

Caroline nodded slowly, biting the inside of her cheek before she sighed. "You didn't like when I took Abbie school shopping without discussing it with you first, last year. Or whenever anything like that happens, so I've been a little," she looked down a little, scuffing her socked toe at the floor, adorably. "Worried, I guess." She pinched the bridge of her nose, "I mean, Abbie's not necessarily *wrong*. It's not really my place to–"

"It is your place," the words escaped Hannah faster than either of them expected it.

Caroline stared at her for a long moment.

Hannah stared back at Caroline, surprised by herself, if the pounding of her heart was any evidence.

"It is?" Caroline asked, shock evident in her tone.

"I…" Hannah licked her lips as she let out a small, baffled laugh and pushed a hand through her hair. "Caroline, you are the only other real parental figure Abbie has. You're there for her whenever she needs you, no matter what is happening between you and I. You've stepped up for her in a way that no one else has, other than me, just because you're – you. Abbie spends nearly as much time with you as she does me, maybe more sometimes. You aren't just some glorified babysitter." The rightness of the words settled comfortably inside of Hannah, bolstering her. "It *is* your place."

Caroline absolutely gaped at her for a few seconds before she recovered and a smile bloomed over her face. It was a smile of such pure wonder, Hannah was so proud for having caused it.

A few seconds later, Caroline shook her head. "But, Abbie's so angry–"

"Sweetheart? She's eleven." Hannah walked closer, close enough to look Caroline right in the eye as she reached up and cupped that perfect jawline so that Caroline would look at her and see how much she meant this. "You have a relationship with Abbie where you're mostly friends, and that's great. Abbie knows the rules and, frighteningly, has figured out the whole parenting system where she knows she is going to have a better time with us when she follows them. But it doesn't mean she always does. You just haven't had to deal with it before because you're her best buddy."

"It's a shitty feeling," Caroline grumbled but leaned into Hannah's hands.

She stroked her thumbs delicately over the soft skin of Caroline's cheeks as she agreed, "It is. And you did the hard part of parenting for the first time, fantastically. I'll finish it up for you."

She leaned down to kiss Caroline quickly, wanting to impart a little bit of comfort, before striding back to the door and opening it.

Unsurprised to see Abbie standing outside – she'd deliberately been quick because she knew her daughter was a sneak – she set her firm face on as she arched an eyebrow at Abbie. "Did you give Caroline a hard time today over doing your book report?"

Abbie was quiet but chewed on her bottom lip – an instant guilty tell – for a long moment before she shrugged both of her shoulders up, defiantly. "We were supposed to do decorations! My book report isn't due for *days*."

Hannah put her hands on her hips as she walked over to her daughter and bent down to get on her level, her voice low but stern, "Well, your biggest mistake today was talking to Caroline so poorly. When Caroline asks you to do something – like your homework – do you *really* think it's any different than when I ask you to do it?"

Abbie's face fell and the defiance that was there slowly slipped into a sad, tired frown as she admitted, "No."

She could tell that Abbie was being genuine. Especially as she reached up and rubbed at her tired eyes with a fist in a manner that was very similar to her much younger self that Hannah sometimes missed.

Yeah, whole-weekend sleepovers might have to be re-thought for the time being with this kind of lack of sleep.

Hannah gave Abbie a little nod and reached out to put her hands on Abbie's shoulders. "Why don't you go up to your room and have a little time to yourself to reflect, rest, and prepare the rest of your report while dinner's cooking? And think about the apology you want to give Caroline, too."

"Can I have my cookie from the advent calendar first?" Abbie gave her an expectant look.

Hannah opened her mouth to answer – *no* – before she caught herself. This one, for the first time in Abbie's life, wasn't her call; after all, she hadn't purchased that calendar. "I don't know, what did Caroline say?"

That deferment felt odd, she'd admit. But it didn't feel *wrong*, and she marveled at that.

Abbie's blue eyes rolled before she let out a big sigh. "She said I can't have it until after dinner, now."

"Then, I guess we know the answer to that, don't we?"

Abbie reluctantly nodded, sighed, and started up the stairs. Hannah watched her go for a moment, before she turned around to give Caroline a little smile, as she met those dark eyes that had watched the entire interaction.

She didn't know how to express all of the feelings that sat inside of her, as she registered the weight of them.

Caroline still looked a bit shell-shocked as she poked her head through the doorway from which she'd clearly watched the entire interaction. "I–"

The rest of what she was going to say was stolen by Hannah's mouth and a surprised squeal – very not-Caroline-like, Hannah thought, as she smiled against those full lips, and deepened the kiss by sliding her tongue into Caroline's mouth.

Hannah didn't know how to put it into words.

This feeling that sat inside of her with Caroline and Abbie this evening – that Caroline had now seen and dealt with Abbie on a bad day, and she did it in a way Hannah herself would have. That even if neither of them realized it, Abbie had reached a point with Caroline where she was able to let herself express defiance, without being afraid that Caroline wouldn't be there at the end of it.

She knew for damn sure that Abbie didn't have tantrums or defiance or attitude toward Michael – maybe in a few years, it might happen, but Hannah knew enough about her daughter's subconscious, had done enough reading, and talking about it with her own therapist to know that Abbie would never push Michael away, due to the deeply rooted fear that he wouldn't be there *at all* anymore if she did.

And most of all, she realized as she pulled back from the kiss – but only far enough to look into Caroline's eyes in her own shock – that sharing the parenting of Abbie with Caroline, Hannah's most precious and prided aspect of her adulthood identity, didn't make her feel less at all.

It didn't make her feel afraid or worried or codependent.

It made her feel like things were... right.

December 25 – This Year

"*For* as much as I love my nieces and nephews, I've definitely never given my siblings the credit they deserve on Christmas," Caroline murmured against Hannah's ear through a yawn as they sat back on the couch as Abbie finished opening her gifts.

Hannah turned an amused smile on her girlfriend, enjoying her tousled dark locks that she still hadn't brushed since waking up a couple of hours ago. "Aren't you the pro when it comes to kids?"

Caroline groaned as she leaned her head back, "Yes, and don't you forget it," she poked her finger into Hannah's side, before she let her hand fall to Hannah's thigh and settled in a light, warm touch. "However, I am *not* a pro when it comes to Christmas."

"This, I know," Hannah agreed. "But you've held your own."

"I would hope so! Up until one finishing up everything for Christmas morning, and then woken up at seven… I even ate half of Santa's cookies," Caroline shot a lazy, charming grin her way, before she sat up to tell Hannah in a serious whisper, "And still, it was the best Christmas I've had by far."

Nerves edged into Hannah's stomach and she bit her lip, searching those dark eyes, "Yeah?"

Caroline nodded. "Yeah."

"Better than last year?" Hannah asked, initially teasing, but – actually genuinely questioning.

"Last year was the best at the time," Caroline acknowledged with a grin, "You kissing me in front of Ab was… it was special. But having you two here all night with me was better."

Abbie had announced that she wanted to spend Christmas Eve over at Caroline's house when they'd finished decorating her tree together last week. And Hannah – well, she'd had a lot to consider and think about in the last few weeks, but that aligned closely with what she wanted, she'd found.

She wanted to spend the holidays here. In the house she designed. With the woman she loved. In the place her daughter felt at home. She wanted to be here on most of her days. On… all of her days.

And while that was terrifying to admit to herself on one hand, it was also liberating.

The only thing she had left to do, was tell it to Caroline. But did she tell it? Or – ask it? Caroline had made no secret of the fact that she wanted this – wanted them. Permanence, promises, and future.

All of that definitely included living together.

But other than the few – tense. Because of Hannah, but still – moments of conversation about key exchanges and the future, Caroline had never really expressly asked Hannah to move in.

In fact, she'd expressly said that she *wasn't* asking.

So, how did Hannah go about bringing that up? How the hell did someone ask to move in with their partner?

It had been on Hannah's mind prominently for the last few weeks, because she felt so out of her depth. The only thing she had managed to do was have a talk with Abbie over dinner last week around how she might feel about moving in with Caroline at some point.

The affirmative excitement she was met with was resounding and entirely unsurprising.

Even though it had made sense to her at the time to ensure that Abbie was comfortable with the possibility of living with Caroline in the near future, she now wondered if her mistake was not discussing it first with Caroline. If only because of the sheer amount of times she'd been asked since that conversation *when! When! When!*

When, indeed.

"Hey," Caroline's voice brought her out of her head, concerned eyes trained on her face. "You okay?"

"Yeah!" She coughed, rolling her eyes at her own breathy, unconvincing tone.

The dubious look on Caroline's face reflected how she felt.

Was this the right time? The thought bounced around her mind. Late Christmas morning in their pajamas, while Abbie combed through the gifts on the floor. Hannah hadn't really had many moments in life that she planned for the right time.

Her mom had died before she'd seen sixty-five, and Hannah hadn't been ready. The stick had turned pink when she'd only been twenty-one, and Hannah hadn't been ready. Michael had fooled her and manipulated her into a whole marriage and life no one could possibly ever be ready for. She'd left Michael with no real plans in place and had scrambled for stability, not ready at all.

Even falling for Caroline, as amazing and beautiful as it was… Hannah hadn't been *ready*.

"Seriously, what is it?" Caroline asked, turning to face her.

Hannah searched those dark eyes, eyes that made her feel safe, and opened her mouth, trying to find the right words.

She only struggled for a few moments before Abbie popped up to stand in front of them. A large green bow from one of her gifts was stuck onto the top of sleep-messy blonde hair from when Caroline had stuck it there over an hour ago, and she was holding a box.

A rather large box that Hannah definitely did not recognize, messily wrapped in the way that Abbie wrapped gifts.

She deposited the box on Caroline's lap and bounced on the balls of her feet.

Hannah arched an eyebrow at her. "How did you get that box here without me seeing it? I didn't bring that with our other gifts."

"I found the box here, in the basement from all of the boxes that Caroline used to move," Abbie explained, biting her lip before she urged Caroline to open.

Caroline shot her a questioning look, before she slowly unwrapped the box. Hannah leaned in close to peer over her shoulder as she flipped open the cardboard flaps and revealed…

"Are these… your clothes?" Caroline asked, sounding just as puzzled as Hannah felt, as she picked up a blue T-shirt that was most definitely Abbie's and held it up. She let out a little laugh, holding the shirt up to herself. "I don't think it's really going to fit, but I appreci–"

"It's stuff I'm bringing with me to move in!" Abbie informed her excitedly.

Oh, boy. Hannah dug two fingers into her temple and rubbed, hard, as she figured… she shouldn't be surprised.

Caroline seemed at her own loss for words, the shirt laying crumpled on her lap as she looked between Hannah, the box, and Abbie, then back. She finally shook her head, giving Abbie a smile that Hannah could tell was a little forced. "I, uh, think your mom would miss you."

Abbie shook her head. "No! She's coming too! We want to move in!"

Hannah's cheeks burned as she shook her head. "Ab, you can't – we can't just *say* we want to move in."

Caroline whipped her head to look at Hannah. "We? *We?* Want to? You want to?"

"Someone has to say it!" Abbie gestured wildly.

Caroline didn't take her eyes off of Hannah. Wide, hopeful, confused, and questioning, they bore into Hannah's own and demanded an answer.

"I just… there's not much in my life that I've had the luxury of waiting until I was ready. It's all been a series of moments that I'm thrust into and I manage them the best I can. And I think…" She dragged her hands through her hair, shrugging with a deep breath and ridiculous butterflies in her stomach. "I think I needed that, for once. The time to feel like I was ready. Like I *am* ready."

"And, you do? You feel like you're ready?" Caroline asked, sounding breathless, a bright, hopeful expression Hannah *adored* on her face. "Don't play any Christmas pranks on me or anything, you know this day and I have a tenuous relationship already."

A laugh escaped through Hannah's lips, pushing through the nerves, her heart beating a little too fast. "I wouldn't. Not about something like this."

Not something that mattered so much.

She only had time to let out a surprised exhale as Caroline snaked an arm around her waist and pulled her in for a kiss. Hannah sighed into it, immediately reaching up to trace her fingers over Caroline's jaw. The sharp lines that started it all, really.

The thought made her smile against Caroline's lips, and the smile didn't dissipate at all, as she distantly heard Abbie gleefully whoop.

No, it wasn't a proposal, it wasn't marriage, it wasn't the promise of *always*. Not yet.

But for Hannah, it was as good as. This was the first step toward a new forever. One that she actually thought could be even better than she'd ever expected.

Other Books by Haley Cass:

Those Who Wait

Sutton Spencer's ideas for her life were fairly simple: finish graduate school and fall in love. It would be a lot simpler if she could pinpoint exactly what she should do when she graduates in less than a year. Oh, and if she could figure out how to talk to a woman without feeling completely hopeless, that would be great too.

Charlotte Thompson is very much the opposite. She's always had clear steps outlining her path to success with no time or inclination for romance. Her burgeoning career in politics means everything to her and she's not willing to compromise it for something as insignificant as love. Fleeting, casual, and discreet worked perfectly fine.

When they meet through a dating app, it's immediately clear that they aren't suited for anything more than friendship. Right?

When You Least Expect It

Caroline Parker knows three things to be true. First, she is going to be Boston's most sought after divorce attorney by thirty-five. Second, given how terrible her romantic track record is, falling in love isn't in the cards for her. And third, Christmas only brings her bad luck - being broken up with not once, not twice, but three times during the holidays is proof enough of that.

When she runs into Hannah Dalton on Christmas Eve, she has no reason to believe her luck will change. After all, though Hannah is probably the most gorgeous woman she's ever seen, she's also straight. And married to Caroline's work rival.

While being hired by Hannah throws her for a loop, winning a divorce case and sticking it to her ex-colleague should be enough of a thrill. But as the months slip by, bringing her closer to both Hannah and her adorable daughter Abbie, the lines between attorney and client begin to blur. And she could have never predicted just how much she wants them to.

In the Long Run

Free-spirited and easygoing Taylor Vandenberg left her hometown of Faircombe, Tennessee as soon as she could, and in the twenty-five years since, she has rarely looked back. She wouldn't change anything about how her life has turned out –

having traveled to nearly every country, never staying anywhere long enough to feel stifled. Very few things can hold her attention back in Faircombe: her sister/best friend, her precocious niece, and perhaps the prospect of riling up Brooke Watson.

Brooke has known Taylor for her entire life, given that her best friend is Taylor's younger brother. And a lifelong knowledge of Taylor means that Brooke knows she's trouble: irresponsible, takes nothing seriously, and is irritatingly attractive. Unlike Taylor, Brooke loves their town so much that she's spent her adult life dedicated to making sure it doesn't get swept away like many of the other declining small cities of the American South. Faircombe means the world to her, and she's willing to do just about anything to make sure it flourishes.

Even if it means working with Taylor, whose path seems to continuously be crossing with Brooke's everywhere she turns…

Down to A Science

Ellie Beckett's life is simple and uncomplicated; she's on track to become a leading expert in biomedical engineering, she has a pub where she feels comfortable enough to hang out multiple times a week, and, so what if she doesn't have time for… people? She doesn't need or want them.

Until she meets Mia Sharpe.
As it turns out, maybe Ellie does want at least one person.

About the Author

Haley lives in Massachusetts, where she has a love/hate relationship with the weather extremities but would also hate to live somewhere without fall foliage. She spends most of her time watching too much television and thinking about the future. Oh, and writing.

Her mother likes to talk about the time she wrote her first story while sitting under the kitchen table for privacy. Twenty years later, she still likes to write but is slightly too tall to sit under the kitchen table.